CRY, MOTHER SPAIN

LYDIE SALVAYRE

CRY, MOTHER SPAIN

Translated from the French by Ben Faccini

MACLEHOSE PRESS
QUERCUS · LONDON

First published in the French language as *Pas pleurer* by Éditions du Seuil, Paris in 2014
First published in Great Britain in 2016
This paperback edition published in 2017 by

MacLehose Press
An imprint of Quercus Publishing Ltd
Carmelite House
50 Victoria Embankment
London EC4Y 0DZ

An Hachette UK company

This book has been selected to receive financial assistance from English PEN's
"PEN Translates" programme, supported by Arts Council England. English PEN
exists to promote literature and our understanding of it, to uphold writers' freedoms
around the world, to campaign against the persecution and imprisonment of writers
for stating their views, and to promote the friendly co-operation of writers and
the free exchange of ideas. www.englishpen.org

A CIP catalogue record for this book is available
from the British Library.

ISBN (MMP) 978 0 85705 452 4
ISBN (Ebook) 978 0 85705 451 7

10 9 8 7 6 5 4 3 2 1

Designed and typeset in Haarlemmer by Libanus Press Ltd, Marlborough
Printed and bound in Great Britain by Clays Ltd, St Ives plc

Translator's Note

I am indebted to a number of people for their advice with this translation. Above all I would like to thank the author for her guidance in helping me understand the complex personal and historical threads in her book and for giving me precious insight into the hybrid French-Spanish spoken by the main character, Montse.

A range of engaging characters inhabit the book alongside Montse and each one, in his or her own way, is emblematic of a faction in the opening months of the Spanish Civil War. I have included a glossary to make these warring political and military organisations as clear and distinct as possible.

I would like to thank William Fiennes, Roland Chambers, Gala Sicart, María Victoria García Benavides, James Phillips, Nicole Hubbard, and my wife, Emily, for their ideas and suggestions – and Christopher and Koukla MacLehose for first introducing me to this book.

BEN FACCINI
London, 2016

Author's Preface

In 2012 I read *Les Grands Cimetières sous la lune* by the French writer Georges Bernanos (1888–1948). I was shocked by it, indeed so shocked that I ended up writing *Pas pleurer*, translated in its English edition as *Cry, Mother Spain*.

In his book, Bernanos describes the Francoist atrocities he witnessed in the opening months of the Spanish Civil War in 1936. In many cases, these crimes were carried out with the complicity of the clergy.

The book was published in France in 1938 and caused an immediate uproar. The diehards on the right accused Bernanos of betrayal, while the left-wing intelligentsia praised him to the skies, perhaps not fully understanding his stance.

Bernanos refused to be pinned down by anyone, however. Exponents of both right and left would never succeed in claiming his work as their own. Though he declared himself to be passionately Catholic and a monarchist, his freedom of spirit meant he eschewed all labels, prejudices and ideologies.

Bernanos is not read much in France nowadays and remains largely unknown abroad. Is it because he was a solitary writer and so hard to categorise? Is it because he refused to mould himself to the attitudes of his time? I don't know. I'm just delighted English-language readers will now get the chance to discover his writing through my book.

LYDIE SALVAYRE
Paris, 2016

What art thou afraid of, cowardly creature? What art thou weeping at, heart of butter-paste?

¿De qué temes, cobarde criatura? ¿De qué lloras, corazón de mantequillas?

CERVANTES, *Don Quixote*, II, 29
(translated by John Ormsby, 1885)

I

In the name of the Father, and of the Son, and of the Holy Spirit.
A ceremonial ring on his venerable hand, the Most Reverend
Archbishop of Palma pointed at the chests of the "guilty poor",
singling them out to the vigilante firing squads. This is how the
writer Georges Bernanos reported it; a fervent Catholic told it
this way.

Spain, 1936. The Civil War was about to erupt. The "guilty
poor" were those who dared open their mouths, and on July 18,
1936, my mother opened her mouth for the first time. She was
fifteen. She lived up in the hills, cut off from the world, in a
village where wealthy landowners had kept families like hers in
the most abject poverty for centuries.

At the same time, Georges Bernanos' own son was getting
ready to fight in the Madrid trenches, dressed in the blue Falangist
uniform. For a few weeks, Bernanos believed his son's enlist-
ment in the Nationalist forces was justified. Bernanos' views
were known to all. He had been a militant for *Action Française*,
an admirer of Drumont. He declared himself a monarchist, a

Catholic, a scion of traditional French values, closer in spirit to what he termed the "working-class aristocracy" than the moneyed bourgeoisie he loathed. In Spain, at the time of the generals' uprising against the Republic, Bernanos took a while to gauge the scale of the unfolding disaster, but he had soon to accept the evidence he saw around him. The Nationalists were carrying out a systematic purge of suspects and, between killing sprees, Catholic dignitaries were granting them absolution *in the name of the Father, and of the Son, and of the Holy Spirit.* The Spanish Church had become the executioners' whore.

Helpless, Bernanos watched this vile connivance take hold. He realised with painful clarity that he had to break with his old sympathies and note everything down, become a reluctant witness.

He was one of only a handful from his political camp to show such courage.

> *A mis soledades voy,*
> *De mis soledades vengo.**
>
> *I go to and from my solitudes.*

On July 18, 1936, my mother, accompanied by my grandmother, was introduced to the Burgos family, the *señores* who wished to employ a new maid – the previous one having been sent home because she smelled of onions. When it came to pronouncing a

---

* Lope de Vega, "La Dorotea", 1632

final verdict on my mother, don Jaime Burgos Obregón turned to his spouse with a satisfied look. He studied my mother from head to toe, and stated with an air of assurance that my mother has never forgotten: *She seems quite humble.* My grandmother thanked him as if he were congratulating her, *But that comment,* my mother says, *throws me into turmoil. For me it's an insult, a patada in the arse, a kick in the culo, it makes me leap ten metros within my own head, it jolts my brain which had been slumbering for more than fifteen years. It makes me understand the meaning of the words my brother José had just brought back from the Anarchist communes around Lérida. So when we are in the street again, I start to shriek, to griter: "She seems quite humble"! Do you realise what he meant? Keep your voice down, your grandmother implored me; she was a woman who liked to keep a low profile. What don Jaime means – I was really boiling, my darling, ma chérie, I was boiling with rage – is that I will make a good maid, sweet and thick, and obedient with it. It means I will accept doña Sol's orders without flinching, that I will clean up her shit without protest. It means I seem to have all the qualities of an idiot, and I won't balk at anything, I won't cause any sort of moleste to anyone. It means don Jaime will pay me, how do you say it? clopinettes, peanuts, and I'll have to say muchísimas gracias with my sweet, grateful, humble face. Oh Lord, your grandmother whispered to herself, looking alarmed, keep your voice down, they'll hear you. So I begin to shriek, even louder: I don't care if they hear me. I don't want to be some dim maid for the Burgos family, I'd rather go and be a whore in town. For heaven's sake, your grandmother begged me, don't say such terrible things. They didn't even invite us to sit down, I tell her indignantly, they didn't even bother shaking our hands, I remember it clearly, I do remember, because I had an inflammation on the tip of my thumb, I'd bandaged it up – a panadis, isn't it called? – oh, a panaris, a whitlow, is that even a word? If you say so – but don't keep on correcting me or I'll never finish. Anyway, so, your grandmother, to shut me up, her voice all hushed, told me about the considerable benefits awaiting me if I got the job as a maid: I'd be housed, fed, and kept clean, and I'd have time off every Sunday to go and dance the jota in the church square, and I'd even get a small stipend and a little yearly bonus to build up a dowry, maybe even put some money aside. At these words I say: I would prefer to die, dying would be better, plutôt morir. Oh, heavens above, your grandmother whispered, even more quietly this time, throwing nervous glances at the houses along the street. And I started to run at full vélocité towards my attic room. By sheer good fortune, war broke out the next day and I never went to work as a maid for the Burgos family, or for anyone else for that matter. The war, ma chérie, came in the nick of time.*

My mother had been watching television that evening and the random image of a man interviewing the president of France had abruptly reminded her of her brother José's enthusiasm on his return from Lérida. His impatience and new-found revolutionary zeal had made him seem so handsome. And it came back to my mother in one fell swoop: don Jaime Burgos Obregón's little remark, the elation of July 1936, the euphoric discovery of city life and the Frenchman she loved so passionately, the man my sister and I have called André Malraux since we were children.

My mother is Montserrat Monclus Arjona, a name I am happy to appropriate and revive for a short while, rescuing it from the oblivion to which it has been consigned. For the time being, I don't want to introduce any invented characters into my account. My mother is my mother. Georges Bernanos is the admired writer of *Les Grands Cimetières sous la lune* and the Catholic Church is the despicable institution it was in 1936.

> *Fuente es mi vida*
> *en que mis obras beben.*

> *My life is a fountain*
> *from which my deeds are nourished.*

My mother was born on March 14, 1921. Her family and friends call her Montse or Montsita. She's ninety years old as she sits and remembers her youth in the crossbred, trans-Pyrenean language she has adopted since Fate hurled her into a village somewhere in the south-west of France more than seventy years ago.

My mother was beautiful once. They tell me she used to have that particular carriage Spanish women had in the old days when they balanced water pitchers on their heads and now only seen in ballet dancers. They tell me she used to move like a boat, its sail upright and supple. They tell me she had the body of a film star and she carried the kindness of her heart in her eyes.

Now she's old, wrinkled, her body decrepit, with a bewildered, unsteady gait. Yet the mention of Spain in 1936 reawakens a youthfulness in her gaze, a light I haven't seen before. She suffers from dementia, and everything she's lived through, from the war to today, has all but vanished. Yet her memories of the summer of 1936, when the unimaginable took place, are still intact. It was a time, she says, when she discovered life – without doubt the only adventure of her existence. Does this mean, therefore, that what my mother took to be reality for the following seventy-five years was somehow not as real? I often think so.

That evening, I listen to her stoking the ashes of her lost youth, and I see her face becoming animated again as if all her *joie de vivre* were gathered up in those few days of the summer of 1936 in the great Spanish city, as if time had stopped still on the calle San Martín, on August 13, 1936, at 8.00 in the morning. I listen to her invoking her memories while my parallel reading of Bernanos' *Les Grands Cimetières sous la lune* fills in any gaps and darkens the picture at the same time. I try to unravel the reasons why the two accounts disturb me so much, and I'm afraid the disturbance will lead me in a direction I have absolutely no intention of taking. More precisely, these memories release contradictory and sometimes confused feelings in me through hidden sluices. Though my mother's rush of freedom in 1936 fills me with a sort of amazement, a childish joy, Bernanos' chronicling of atrocities – his observations of the darkness of men, their hatreds and furies – stirs my fears of seeing today's bastards revive the noxious ideas I thought had been put to rest a long time ago.

On the morning my fifteen-year-old mother, accompanied by my grandmother, applied for the job of maid, doña Pura – sister of the aforementioned don Jaime Burgos Obregón – was sitting bolt upright as usual in her stiff-backed leather chair reading, in a state of ecstasy, the headlines of her newspaper, *Acción Española*: "A young general has decided to take control of eternal Spain as it slides towards democracy and socialism, in the hope of building a dam against the Bolshevik invasion. Other generals have, without a moment's hesitation, rallied around this extraordinary leader of men, and the nation's forces have been reawakened. But will spirit, intelligence, devotion to the national cause and heroism be enough to overcome the base appetites and bestial instincts elevated to the rank of government by Moscow as it sets its sights on poisoning the whole of the European side of the Mediterranean?" The article ended with this question and it threw doña Pura into such a state of alarm that she was overcome by heart palpitations. Doña Pura was prone to palpitations, and even though the doctor had ordered her to avoid all sources of vexation, her patriotism meant that she couldn't stop reading the Nationalists' paper. *It's my duty*, she told the doctor in a faltering voice.

Over the following days, doña Pura lived in constant dread of her house being pillaged, her land stolen and her fortune plundered by a band of thieves led by Montse's brother José. Maruca, the grocer's wife, had confided in her how the Anarchists carried out their bloody hold-ups, raping and eviscerating nuns, sullying their convents with abominable desecrations. Doña Pura imagined them bursting into her own bedroom, ripping down the ivory crucifix watching over her immaculate white bed, stealing her enamel-encrusted jewellery box and giving themselves over to the most unspeakable abuses. Despite this, she continued to greet the parents of the village hotheads when she came across them. She really had a good heart.

But come night-time, kneeling at her *prie-dieu*, she beseeched the Lord to protect her family from these savages who had no respect for anyone.

May they die and go to hell!

No sooner had she uttered this pronouncement than she blushed with shame. Might the Lord, undoubtedly endowed with exceptional powers, have heard her words? She would have to confess to don Miguel (the village priest who had not yet fled) the following morning. He would prescribe three *Ave Marias* and a *Pater Noster*. These had the same medicinal effect on her conscience as a dose of aspirin. It was well known that whatever crime the Catholics committed against the Reds – whether by blade, gun, club or iron rod – they were immediately exonerated and forgiven as long as the criminal showed contrition in time for evening prayer. Such arrangements with the Spanish heavens could be truly magical.

Doña Pura resumed her prayer and pleaded with the Holy Virgin Mary to put an end to the actions of the brazen fools insulting her God. Taking a swipe at her wealth was an insult to the Lord. She understood better than anyone what constituted an insult to God. She was, in fact, what people in the village, thanks to an eloquent linguistic shortcut, called a *facha*. When the word is pronounced with the Spanish *ch*, it is accompanied by a spit.

There were a few *fachas* in the village and what united these fascists was the belief that:

THE ONLY GOOD RED
IS A DEAD RED

My uncle José, Montse's brother, was a Red, or rather a Red-and-Black.

He'd been fuming with anger since his sister recounted her visit to the Burgos household.

The Reds in 1936 were always cross, even more so when they were both Red and Black. José thought his sister had been insulted. Spain in 1936 was brimming over with insulted people.

"She seems quite humble"? "She seems quite humble"! Who does the bastard think he is? He'll regret it, the barefaced cabrón. I'll teach that bourgeois to think twice before opening his mouth again.

José had been transformed by his time in Lérida. His eyes were filled with light from the heavenly marvels he had seen. His mouth spouted words from another world, to the point where his mother said, *They've gone and changed my son.*

Every year, between harvesting the almonds in May and the

hazelnuts in September, José worked as a hired hand cutting hay on a vast estate near Lérida. The job tested the limits of his endurance and paid a pittance, but he happily gave the money to his parents.

From the age of fourteen, José's days had been consumed by work in the fields, from dawn till dusk. His life was regulated by it. He hadn't thought to question his existence or dream for a second that things could be different.

Yet when he arrived in Lérida, with his friend Juan, he discovered a city that had been shaken up to the point of dizziness. Its moral codes had been turned upside down, its surrounding farmlands had been collectivised and its churches transformed into cooperatives. Cafés buzzed with rallying calls, everyone laughed with happiness. He'd never forget the excitement and the emotion of it.

José discovered words so new and so bold that his young soul became enraptured by them. These were immense words, grandiose, etched in fire, sublime, words for a new era: *Revolución! Comunidad! Libertad!* When shouted with the stress at the end, they were like a punch to the face.

José was as filled with wonder as a child.

Things he'd never thought about before began to fill his mind.

Immeasurable things.

He learned to raise his fist and sing "Hijos del Pueblo".

He chanted *Down with Oppression, Long live Freedom.* And *Death to Death.*

He felt alive. He felt he was the best. He felt modern, his heart bursting. He understood what it was to be young. He'd had no idea before. He said he could have died without ever realising it. He saw how dull and diluted his past desires had been.

He identified in this vast black gasp of life something he called poetry, since he had no other word for it.

He returned to the village with his mouth overflowing with grand phrases, a red-and-black scarf round his neck. With impassioned eloquence, he told his audience (limited for the time being to his mother and sister) that a new dawn was rising (he had a natural propensity for lyricism), that Spain had at last become properly Spanish and he too even more so. Shaking with intensity, he said *the old order which perpetuated servitude and shame was on the point of being destroyed; the revolution of hearts and minds had begun and it would soon spread to the entire country, and, one thing leading to another, to the whole universe.* He said *money would no longer decide all things, it would no longer be the basis for distinctions between people and soon* –

The sea will taste of sweet aniseed, his mother interrupted, annoyed.

– *and soon there will no more injustice, no more hierarchy, no more exploitation, no more wretchedness, and people will be able to* –

Go on holiday with the Pope, his mother interrupted again, exasperated.

– *share their riches, and those who have shut their mouths since they were born, those who lease land from that cabrón don Jaime*

21

who owns every centimetre of it, those who clean up his wife's shit
and piss and scour her toilet –

Not again! his mother said, she'd had enough already.

– they will rise up, they will fight, they will free themselves of all
tyranny –

I'll bloody give you tyranny, his mother exploded. *It's seven in*
the evening and you'd better see to the hens. I've prepared their bucket.

But José still had so much to say, and the hens, impervious to
Bakunin's philosophies, were going to have to wait a bit longer
for their feed.

Since returning from Lérida, José was bursting with an inexhaustible stream of ideas. Sometimes he was raging – sprinkling
his sentences with swear words (*coño, joder* and dozens of
puñetas) – other times he was simply elated.

In the morning he railed against the bad rich – *a pleonasm if*
ever there was one, as the rich could only be bad (he discovered the
word "pleonasm" in the *Tierra y Libertad* newspaper). *What for-*
tune, he asked, *had not been stolen?* He ranted against the profi-
teers, and the friends of don Miguel, the priest, who, for one, was
soon going to feel the cold wind of the revolution (laughs) whis-
tling up his cassock. He ranted against the thief don Jaime Burgos
Obregón and other tight-fisted employers and landowners, but
most of all he raged against the leader of the Nationalist gang
who had hoisted himself up to become leader of the rebellion:
General Francisco Franco Bahamonde. He insulted Franco in
language some might term vulgar –calling him *a dwarf priest-*

fucker, a pile of shit, a filthy son of a whore, a murderer he'd string up by the balls – or he described him, in the rhetoric of logico-political Bakuninian thought, as *the ally-by-default of capitalism, the enemy of the proletariat, themselves victims twice over of the Republican government's distrust and Francoist repression.*

Even if José's heart was a tinderbox in the morning, by evening he was once again dreaming of fabulous things and he promised his sister Montse a world where *no-one would be the servant or property of another – where no-one would be deprived of their natural entitlement to sovereignty because of another* (a phrase taken from the newspaper *Solidaridad Obrera*), *a fair and beautiful world, a paraíso,* and he laughed with happiness at such a paradise *where love and work would freely cohabit, in joy, and where –*

I don't see how that's going to happen, Montse interrupted him, trying not to laugh. *How can I pick olives in January, freely and with joy, when my fingers are frozen and my back is racked with pain? You're dreaming,* she told him, with all the brashness of a fifteen-year-old.

Her comment momentarily derailed José's glowing promises, yet he got going again with the same ardour as before. And Montse was happy to hear her brother imagine a future where no-one would spit on anyone, where there would be no more fear or shame, where women would be the equals of men.

Equal in nastiness too? Montse asked mischievously.

Equal in everything, including nastiness, José said.

Montse smiled. Her entire being secretly agreed with José

23

because he knew how to attach words to unspoken ideas, opening up new realms to her, as unknown and huge as a city.

She prodded her brother to keep him going. He began to speak like a philosopher (it was the side of José she preferred), and he launched into a florid speech on the art of dispossession. Montse: *The art of what?* José: *Dispossession.* Montse: *What's that?* José: *It means that owning an object, a house, a jewel, a wristwatch, mahogany furniture, qué sé yo? who knows? anything, is to make yourself a slave to that object, it means that you want to keep it at all costs, it adds new servitude to the enslavements you cannot escape. But in the free communes we're going to set up, everything will belong to us and nothing will belong to us at the same time, do you get it? The land will belong to us like the light and air, but it will not be owned by anyone.* José was jubilant. *Our houses will be without locks or bolts, don't you see?* Montse drank in his words, only fully understanding about a quarter of them. They did her good without her knowing why. Their tired mother hoped these fantasies, which seemed peculiar to youth, would last only a short while and José would quickly come back down to earth – to her, that meant abandoning all dreams. It was her secret wish, and the secret wish of all the mothers in the village. Mothers are monsters. *We're going to lead the revolution and crush the Nationalists,* José shouted ecstatically. *Out with the Nationalists! Out! Out! Fuera!*

In Palma, in Majorca, where Bernanos was staying, the Nationalists had already begun hunting down the Reds, even though on that tranquil island they had only belonged to moderate parties and not taken part in the massacre of priests.

Since the start of this holy war, since the *Santa Guerra* had been declared – since the Fascist aeroplanes had been blessed by the Archbishop of Palma, robed in full ceremonial splendour, since the baker's wife had started giving him the Mussolini salute every time they met, since the café owner, puce with indignation, had told him the farm workers who had dared to request better pay for their fifteen-hour days should be dispatched with a bullet to the head – Bernanos had felt a burgeoning anxiety take hold of him.

Sept, the French Catholic magazine run by the Dominicans, had agreed to publish his regular eyewitness accounts of the events in Spain. These chronicles make up the bulk of *Les Grands Cimetières sous la lune*.

Some days, walking in the countryside surrounding Palma, Bernanos would come across a corpse at the edge of a dirt track, swarming with flies, head bloodied, face slashed, eyelids bulging with bruises, the open mouth pitch black. At first he supposed these summary executions were blunders, or acts of revenge everyone would repudiate. He believed the fire would quickly die out, but the flames spread, and so did his distress.

A fire of another kind was burning its way through José's spirit. He raged and rejoiced in equal measure, all day long. Yet as soon as his father returned from the fields, José hid away in silence. His father was the owner of an eight-hectare field, passed down from one generation to the next, which he had enlarged by buying a few plots from don Jaime, one instalment at a time. This parched earth, capable only of supporting a few spindly olive trees and patches of depleted grass – just enough to feed goats – was his only heritage, his most precious asset, probably more precious than his wife, even though he'd chosen her with the same care as he'd chosen his mule.

José knew there was no use in trying to persuade his father of the merits of sharing the arable land more equitably. His father, who had never left his dump of a village, who couldn't read or write, and who, according to José, was still stuck in his backward ways, violently rejected his son's ideas, refused to even accept their fundamental validity.

He said: *As long as I'm alive, no-one will come and steal my bread.*

Why couldn't he understand that new ideas were on the brink of changing the world?

His father wasn't interested. He wanted nothing to do with it. *They won't get me*, he said, *I'm not stupid. I wasn't born yesterday*. His standpoint, he maintained, was dictated by ancient peasant wisdom, and the far-sightedness of those who didn't allow themselves to be led astray by tall stories. That was the only valid position to have. His son would do well to follow in his footsteps – and accept a destiny similar to the one breaking his own back. José had a word to qualify such an attitude: "DESPOTIC".

DESPOTIC was another much-used term José had

brought back from Lérida (along with a collection of further words ending in -IC and -ISM).

Despotic father, despotic religion, despotic Stalin, despotic Franco, despotic women and despotic money.

Montse also liked the word and was dying to use it. So when her friend Rosita came to collect her, as on every Sunday, to go and dance the *jota* in the church square, she said she would prefer not to indulge in such a DESPOTIC custom again.

If you like, Rosita said, only vaguely understanding the new word, *but it may be the only opportunity you're going to get to see your boyfriend.*

What boyfriend?

Don't be stupid. Everyone knows about your novio.

Everyone but me.

Diego is mad about you.

Shut up, Montse said, sticking her fingers in her ears.

And now my mother spends her days sitting in a green chair especially designed for invalids, watching the children in the nearby school playground through the window – one of her last remaining pleasures. I feed, wash, dress and walk her, like a child, since she can only move when gripping hold of my arm. Yet my mother can still see herself, once again, hopping in anticipation, running up the calle del Sepulcro towards the church square where a band, *pompompom, pompompom*, is playing a *jota*. *It's the same every Sunday*, my mother says, her face, lined with age, lighting up with childish mischief. *Diego's there, ogling, devouring me with his eyes, giving me the once-over, as you say, and if I look at him he turns from me straight away as if he's been caught red-handed.*

The same circus repeated itself, Sunday after Sunday, under my grandmother's spying gaze, as she had perfectly understood that this merry-go-round of eyes was merely the whirlwind of the heart, *pompompom, pompompom.*

All the mothers of the village formed a ring in the church square to supervise their children, speculating about marriage prospects, *pompompom, pompompom.* Without letting their guard down for a second, the ambitious mothers dreamed of marrying their daughters to the Fabregat boy: *Now he's a real catch.* Most of them, however, limited themselves to wishing their daughter would find a small, comfy nest and a quiet life within the circle of dancers spinning round the pivotal male, though it was not so much a pivot, more a pillar, a pestle, a column, a male obelisk, solidly planted in the village ground, just as it would one day bed itself in the shifting sands of female mystery. *Isn't that just lovely?*

Montse didn't seem at all moved by the silent attention shown by the pivot called Diego.

The redness of his hair repelled her.

His insistence embarrassed her.

He held her in his sights, but it never crossed her mind to respond to his interest. She would sooner have extinguished his flames with cold water.

Despite preparing her dowry like all young girls of her age, and stitching the two enlaced "M"s of her name on white linen sheets and bath towels, Montse didn't share her friends' obsession with quickly finding husbands before she and all the girls were sent off to work as maids (finding a husband was the sole topic of conversation for the young ladies as they skittered up and down the Gran Calle, again and again, up and down: conversations mixed with remarks about so-and-so who stared while pretending not to, and so-and-so who walked past my door three times while my heart thumped full-speed, and so-and-so who wore odd socks – which was not going to get him anywhere, by the way – and Emilio who obviously knew what he was doing, *I'd be careful if I were you. What about Enrique?* At least with him things were more reliable – and other such chirruping, gossiping and warbling).

While Montse was strikingly unflustered by Diego's passion, her brother, José, was not. He had a real problem with Diego setting his heart on his little sister. He found his tricks intolerable. Diego was a *señorito* with a full stomach, a spoilt, overfed child, a daddy's boy and, worst of all, a bourgeois – an armchair revolutionary, who, whether he liked it or not, would always remain a bourgeois. That was enough to be hated.

Since his return from Lérida, José liked to see the world in stark terms.

As for Montse's mother, she was secretly rather pleased the Burgos son was sniffing around her daughter. The young man was well turned out, he was educated, and his family money was compensation enough for the hideous redness of his hair and, indeed, the suspicion he aroused in the village.

Even though they didn't admit it outright, the local people were wary of Diego, the adopted son of don Jaime Burgos Obregón and his wife doña Sol. No-one knew how he'd been conceived or where he'd been born. His parents certainly never talked about how he'd come to be with them, as if they were ashamed of it. And of course no-one dared ask either.

In the village, where all lives were predestined, where you could reliably tell who would become what according to their pedigree, the mystery of Diego's origins led to widespread mistrust – hostility even.

There were the wildest rumours about his parentage. His secretive birth was linked to something dark, painful, slanderous. If the latest rumour was to be believed, Diego was the fruit of an affair between don Jaime and the Filo woman, the village idiot who lived with her elderly witch of a mother, *la Bruja*, in a reconditioned shack on the way out of the village.

No-one knew how the two women survived.

Maybe don Jaime gives them a bit of money, Macario, the village cobbler suggested to Clara.

You mean . . . ? she said, indignantly.

You heard me, the wily cobbler muttered.

What, with . . . ?

Exactly!

Really? Whatever next?

She ditched the cobbler on the spot to spread the news to

Consol, who within five minutes had passed it on to Carmen and so on and so forth.

Everyone knew the rumour was not the least bit true, especially those who spread it. Everyone knew *la Bruja*'s daughter had never been pregnant – such an occurrence would not have gone unnoticed in a small village. Still, the implausible and outrageous tale continued to take hold and find people willing to give it wings. The villagers delighted in it without even believing it, and they tossed in tasty and fanciful titbits, the more sordid the better. *You've got to understand*, my mother says, *gossip was like television in those days, and the villagers gulped it down. They had a romantic thirst for disgrace and drama, it fuelled their dreams, thrilled them.*

But the events of July 1936 gave the rumour greater charge as other more vital matters were now at stake. What was hugely important, desperately and intensely so, in fact, was to classify people as good or bad, according to their political labels. What was crucial was to know who was from the F.A.I., who was from the P.O.U.M., who was from the P.C.E. and who was a Falangist. These allegiances took precedence over everything, obliterating any nuance or contradiction.

All subtleties were abandoned in Spain in 1936.

At this juncture, it's worth noting that a few months earlier and to general astonishment, Diego had joined the Communist party.

Everyone commented on the reasons, and many fell about laughing, imagining the faces doña Pura must have pulled on hearing the news that her nephew had allied himself with the Moscovite monsters. *We got lost in our hypothèses* (my mother's words), *with our cod psychology, as you like to call it. That's what people do when they're deprived of basic entertainment.*

We wondered if Diego had joined the Party to set himself apart from his father, or to safeguard his interests. We wondered whether it was his way of escaping the influence of the Burgos clan or whether it was an emotional response to protect his family from possible reprisals. We wondered whether the real reason wasn't his competition with his father: he wanted to dethrone him and protect him at the same time. We wondered whether he was making up for his childhood in some way, seeking some kind of réparation – we knew nothing about his early years, but we imagined they must have been catastrophic. We wondered whether his joining the Party wasn't the perfect opportunity for him, to allow him to earn his stripes and be accepted by the villagers once and for all. We wondered whether he knew himself why he'd joined the Party and whether the dogmatic way in which he spoke was actually a disguise for his fickleness. We asked ourselves if he worried that the purity of his commitment to the Party might be tainted by his bourgeois background and whether this was leading him to assert his ideas with even greater force.

Diego, who had always been so evasive, so taciturn, now took to talking in the café and elsewhere in the village with an authority and violence that surprised all. He pontificated, put on a show, explained the political situation with all the aplomb of a Robespierre, citing articles from *Mundo Obrero*. He gobbled up its pretentious expressions. He tested them in front of the bedroom mirror. The phrases sounded beautiful and right to him. The confused aspirations which had long troubled his soul had finally found their voice.

Don Jaime didn't recognise his son. It disturbed him. Diego's indoctrination and his idolisation of Stalin were clear evidence that his son's painstakingly long spiritual education had failed.

Since Diego had come to live with his new family, he seemed bent on punishing and upsetting everyone within it. He had always been a gloomy and surly child who refused to be seduced by any form of tenderness, as if some terrible force forbade it.

During adolescence, this turned to an aggressive, baffling resentment, a sort of wordless anger, a simmering hatred for all things and beings. It led those around him to imagine something irreparable had happened in his life even before the torments of adulthood set in. He made deliberately wounding remarks. He had understood the power of words early on. He was precocious that way.

As he didn't dare express the violence he harboured towards his father, he turned on his stepmother instead, sensing a weakness, aware something in her was broken. All doña Sol had to do was speak and Diego immediately took the opposite view. *You're not my mother*, he'd hiss mercilessly at the most insignificant remarks.

You have no rights over me, he'd say, his voice charged with hatred, if she asked him about grammes and kilogrammes or the conjugation of the verbs *ser* and *estar*.

When she kissed him goodnight, he'd wipe his cheek in

ostentatious fashion. All doña Sol could do was bite her lip to stop herself from crying.

It'll end badly, Justina often predicted. (She was the maid doña Pura sacked because she stank of onion, though the real reasons remain a mystery to this day.)

Doña Sol refused to complain to her husband about Diego's behaviour in case it increased the boy's resentment of her. So, inexorably, he gained a greater hold on his stepmother, to the point where he was able to say *Piss off*, *Shut it* or *Fuck you* the moment she spoke to him, with all the cruelty children are capable of.

But what on earth is the matter with you, my darling? doña Sol would ask him with imploring eyes.

I'm not your darling! Diego spat.

So the martyred doña Sol, lips trembling, would keep quiet and hold back her tears.

Don Jaime didn't see, or pretended not to see, his son's hatred for his wife. He worried more about the boy's appalling school results, consoling himself with the thought his son would in any case take over the management of his farmlands one day.

Diego, however, had proclaimed early on that he hated the countryside. With a snarl in his voice, he said he loathed their godforsaken village. It surely held the record for being the most backward in Spain. He had no intention of rotting away there like the rest of the local bumpkins who had no interests in life other than the price of a kilo of olives, the ravages of hailstorms and potential delays to the potato harvest. He didn't want to end up like the farm manager either, who washed himself with eau de cologne every Sunday to quench the stink of manure, or even less El Peque, who smothered his hair in Brylcreem to make up for his lack of shine in other areas of life. He hated the peasants who saw him as a lucky little *señorito* sucking away at his silver spoon. He refused to be a daddy's boy. He wanted to forget his father, forget his birth altogether, forget the illustrious Burgos family and fashion his own path in the world.

Diego's unwillingness to accept his birthright, which was beyond the wildest dreams of most people, offended the simple folk of the village who owned nothing at all. Being odious with his stepmother, and being an introvert, were one thing. What was to be expected anyway of a child who came from nowhere, maybe not even from Spain? And one with red hair like a Dakota Indian to boot. But to refuse to take on his father's land, by far the most fertile and lush fields in the village. *No! no! and no!* The peasants were unanimous about this.

Diego puts on airs. He's too proud.

Where does he get it from?

That's the real question.

They say he stays in bed till nine in the morning, filing his nails and reading Karl Marx.

Who?

Some Russian prophet who wants to string up all the rich bastards like his dad, know what I mean?

He should get up off his arse.

It's none of our business, I suppose.

How old is he now anyway?

Twenty-something.

It's about time he pulled his socks up. You know what they say?
When the worm's already in the fruit, the rot has set in . . .

You only have to look at his . . .

That poor father of his.

The boy's certainly giving him a run for his money!

You can be sure about that.

Yet Diego wasn't ready to forgive the couple he considered to be his fake parents for his calamitous childhood. Their inheritance was an undeserved gift, an inconvenient legacy that crushed him. It forced him to be part of a story in which he had to play the role of interloper. He wanted to be someone, but on his own terms. He wanted to shake off the privileges his bloodline had conferred on him. He refused the idea of being the sole heir even though custom and law dictated that he should devote himself to his father's property, and despite his aunt doña Pura continually telling him – with an overweening smugness he found obscene – that he was a Burgos, in other words a member of a caste, an elite, one of the privileged few. Don Jaime, who had dreamed of Diego perpetuating the family legacy, was profoundly perturbed by it all.

Most of the fathers in the village were unhappy in 1936. Their sons wanted nothing to do with their holy version of Spain and could no longer bear the restrictions foisted on them by the priest, don Miguel. They attempted to free themselves of it by pissing on the geraniums in his garden, or by desecrating the Lord's Prayer during Mass – *Do not give us this day our daily bread, do not forgive us our trespasses as we do not forgive them that trespass against us, do lead us into temptation* . . . They no longer wanted nuns, with skin the colour of candle wax, telling their female pupils that a lusty devil was nestling between their legs. They no longer wanted to work in the fields, earning barely enough to pay for two *copitas*, or rather, to be honest, the six or seven, even the eight or ten glasses they managed to drink on Sunday afternoons at the café run by Bendición and her fat husband. So these sons, who could find no answers to their aspirations in their parents' moribund world, cursed their fathers, rejected their values and hurled mocking and bewildering abuse at them.

History, my daughter chérie, is made of such clashes, such enfrentamientos. No father in the village was safe from these cruel and sad battles, neither Diego's nor José's. Then, my mother adds in language as sophisticated as it is cryptic: *Inherent justice does not obey the decrees of men.*

José's father was all the more disconsolate. His neighbour had just told him his son was cooking up trouble with the local trade unionists, a bunch of hotheads who claimed to be rebels and who strutted around the village with red-and-black scarves tied around their necks. Shame on them!

I'm going to bash his ideas back into place. He'll see what pain's all about, José's father shouted. His son had departed for Lérida a hard-working, respectable, reasonable lad, with his feet firmly on the ground and pointed in the right direction. *And what sort of boy had come back? An excitable, half-loco rebel with his cabeza bursting with stupid ideas.*

It was in Lérida, his father ranted, *that his head got clogged up with all that crap. I'll flush it out of that gullible, snotty-nosed brat, I will, I tell you, I will.*

You'd better get on with it, the neighbour says. *Before he …*

It was in Lérida, the father repeated, *where they fed him all those lies and all that other nonsense: getting rid of money, collectivising the land, sharing out food, a load of barmy ideas. Anyone would think they drugged him.*

And now your son and his friends, the neighbour said, *are going around saying they're about to start a revolution in the village.*

He's an idiot! I'll give him such a hiding.

To cap it all, the neighbour told him how the priest of D., a nearby village, had been found in an olive grove with his skull smashed by a spade, and the sacristan from M. had been discovered beaten to a pulp with a crucifix shoved up his arse. *Who did it? The thugs of the C.N.T., of course.*

Shame on them! José is going to get such a bloody wallop. His father was so overwhelmed by it all he headed straight to the café run by Bendición and her overweight husband. He was going to play dominoes for a while, and knock back a couple of glasses of sweet aniseed, maybe three or four, ten if necessary. He damn well needed to perk himself up a bit, and Bendición's café was the only place in the village where you could get yourself perked up in style. That and the hunters' club.

It was 10.00 at night by the time Father reached home, his spirits high.

He staggered up the stairs, wobbled towards the table and flopped down on his chair.

It was the signal his wife and children had been waiting for to sit down.

Mother brought him his bowl of soup. According to an immutable order, Father was served first, José second, Montse third and Mother last.

Father stank of alcohol.

He regularly drank himself into a stupor.

Words only seemed to come to him when drunk.

That evening, his words, although pasty, coated and slurred, as if all chewed up, were terribly solemn.

Having traced a sign of the cross on the bread with the tip of his knife, he stood and declared – struggling to stay on his feet and without looking anyone in the eye – that he would not tolerate the besmirching of his good name with the irresponsible ideas of the . . . (he attempted to dredge up a dangerous name from the depths of his memory, it took a few seconds) C.N.T. *Everyone be warned, this is a public warning*, he went on, immediately regretting this admonishment as it didn't quite fit with the tragic circumstances of the scene.

Then, with his heavy eyes staring into his bowl of soup, and making a visible effort to focus, he warned he'd not let anyone take the few strips of land he owned to give them to some lazy, incompetent bastard. He slammed his fist down on the table, *¡Y aquí mando yo! I'm in charge here! This is my house.*

Mother grimaced, the way she always did in dramatic situations.

Montse stopped breathing.

José blanched, his chin trembling slightly, but still he said, (and Montse has never forgotten it), *I have never shown you any disrespect* (both José and Montse used the polite form of "you", *usted*, to address their parents)*, but today I ask you to show me some respect.* It was the first time José had stood up to his father, the first time he'd challenged his authority.

Santísimo Jesús, Mother whispered, terrified. An immediate, irrepressible sense of joy swept over Montse.

Father was momentarily disconcerted, but he just repeated in a loud voice: *This is my house. ¡Y aquí mando yo!* – he pointed at the door – *and those who don't like it, they can leave now!*

He plonked himself down to avoid falling over, and added with a touch of majesty: *I rest my arse on your revolution.*

Then he went quiet, his muddled brain refusing to prompt him any more suitable words.

José stood up, pushing his chair to one side.

Father remained anchored to the table, his drunkenness preventing him from moving, and he initiated the awkward manoeuvre of trying to lift his soup-filled spoon. Eventually it reached its intended target after several perilous dips.

Montse and her mother finished their meal, hearts beating wildly, without uttering a word.

I hate that Fascist pig, that facha, José told his sister, as soon as she joined him in the kitchen.

Montse burst out laughing. She found her brother's fits of anger totally hilarious. She couldn't say why.

I wouldn't care if he died, José said.

Don't say that, Montse protested.

I'm going to get out of this shit-hole.

Papa will kill you if you try and leave.

He's a Nazi.

Montse burst out laughing again.

The next day, José was in a good mood once more.

Do you love Jesus? he asked his mother.

What a question! (Mother was busy kneading bread.)

Didn't they tell you in catechism that Jesus was an Anarchist? (José loved to tease her.)

Don't tip the chair, you're going to break it, his mother snapped.

That Jesus said, for instance, that you couldn't serve both God and money.

Careful of the chair! his mother repeated.

That sounds like a typical Anarchist slogan to me.

You're going to break the chair!

Did they tell you that Jesus was also in favour of pooling riches, so that possessions could be shared more equally?

Sweet Mary! Mother shouted. *Stop this nonsense.*

Montse giggled childishly.

Mother switched her gaze from José to Montse, as if searching for the real culprit for such shocking words and behaviour.

What? You're joining in now, too, are you? she said indignantly, looking at her daughter. *What did I do to the Good Lord to deserve this?*

In a renewed bid to convince his mother, José went and fetched the Bible with the cabbage-green spine from his parents' bedroom. He read, in a loud voice: *Acts of the Apostles, II, verses 44–45: The Fellowship of the Believers. "And all who believed were together and had all things in common. And they were selling their possessions and belongings and distributing the proceeds to all, as any had need."*

José looked triumphant.

So? What do you think of that?

Mother looked unsettled.

Nonsense.

It's written in black and white right here in the Bible! José shouted. *It's all here, for fuck's sake. Read it.*

Nonsense, Mother repeated, her face closed.

You're saying the Holy Scriptures are nonsense?

José! Mother screeched, unable to take any more of his blasphemous insinuations.

That's exactly how Catholics are these days! José said, turning to Montse. *But we're going to be even more Catholic than the Cath-*

olics. We're going to create a free commune on former bourgeois lands and properties, I feel divine inspiration for such a task, he said, taking on the beatific look of Saint Thérèse of Lisieux.

Lord help us, Mother sighed. *How much more of this do I have to put up with?*

But this is what the revolution is all about, José said, smiling.

You're going to drive me mad.

Shut up now, Montse said. *Can't you see you're scaring her?*

If they hear you, they'll put you in prison, Mother groaned. She didn't understand anything of the ideas brewing away in her son's head and, for her, acronyms such as C.N.T. and F.A.I. stood for obscure, risky things that led men to fight each other and nothing more.

José burst out laughing.

Montse too.

She had no idea why, but everything her brother said since coming back from Lérida, the very ideas that so angered her father and worried her mother, filled her with utter joy.

Montse and her brother had no knowledge of the appalling crimes Bernanos was witnessing in Palma at the same time. The writer could no longer avoid the evidence he saw around him despite the sympathies he had once had for the old Falange (the organisation founded by Primo de Rivera, which had always been suspicious of the army that had betrayed the king and of the clergy who were "expert in haggling and dealing" – and to which his own son Yves had enthusiastically signed up). Its new version

43

of 1936, however, was being manipulated by a few generals who enjoyed "sowing treachery in their wake" and he could only come to one glaring conclusion: the purge undertaken by these new Nationalists with the foul blessing of the clergy was nothing but blind, systematic Terror.

Still he hesitated to set it down in so many words.

Still he hesitated before making the final leap.

He knew that once he had crossed that line, he would have to see the task through, come what may, and the scale of the undertaking sapped away at his soul. The facts, however, were plain to see: there had not even been five hundred Falangists in Palma before the *pronunciamento* (Franco's uprising). Now, however, Bernanos wrote, "there are fifteen thousand, thanks to a shameless recruitment drive by the soldiers under the orders of an Italian adventurer named Rossi who has turned the Falange into an auxiliary police force in charge of committing atrocities".

This new Falange of 1936 was terrorising the people of Palma. A few days after the *coup d'état*, two hundred inhabitants of the small town of Manacor were deemed suspect and "hauled from their beds in the middle of the night, taken in truckloads to the cemetery, and shot in the head, their corpses piled up and burned". The Most Reverend Archbishop of Palma dispatched one of his cassocked priests to the scene, big shoes paddling around in the blood as he carried out absolutions between rounds of bullets, tracing the sign of the cross in oil on the foreheads of the dead to open up the doors of Heaven. Bernanos noted: "I can only observe that this massacre of defenceless innocents did not lead to a single word of reprimand, nor even a bland sanction from the ecclesiastical authorities. They simply contented themselves with organising thanksgiving processions."

On July 23, 1936, José went to the general assembly held at the town hall, the *ayuntamiento*. He was in belligerent mood. The countdown to revolution had begun. It was time to get serious.

Beforehand he'd gone to fetch his friend Juan, who lived at the top of the calle del Sepulcro – *A road like that*, my mother says, tilting her hand upwards. *With a steep gradient?* I say. *Is that what you mean?* My mother laughs: *Steep gradient? If you like – you've started making up funny words now, haven't you?*

José and Juan had become friends in Lérida. Every summer, from the age of fourteen, they had worked as day labourers on don Tenorio's vast estate, carrying out the same strenuous tasks as the adults around them. It was there that they came across Anarchist ideas and took part in the thrill of setting up an agricultural commune.

They had now turned eighteen.

They had been born in a village where things repeated themselves, identically and endlessly. The rich had their prosperity, the poor their burdens. It was a self-sustaining, suffocating community where the authority of elders was as sacrosanct as the Burgos family wealth, where everyone's life was set in stone from birth, where nothing new ever came along to add hope, not even a small breath of fresh air, a glimpse of life.

José and Juan had grown up isolated from the world, in a village criss-crossed by mournful donkeys, where the only two vehicles were the clapped-out truck Juan's father used to deliver vegetables to town and don Jaime's Hispano-Suiza. It was a lost realm where the first television, the first tractor, even the first motorcycle had yet to make an appearance. The village didn't have a post office and the only doctor lived thirty kilometres away – you cured burns with incantations, and any other illnesses with castor oil and bicarbonate of soda.

So both young men had worked in a slow, slow world, as slow as the plodding village mules, a world where olives were individually picked, where ploughing was done by hand, where jugs were taken to the fountain to be filled with water. They constantly came up against their fathers' authority – fathers who were severe by tradition; believers, by tradition too, in educating their sons with their belts; convinced, by tradition again, that things should forever stay as they were; and resistant to the idea of any father–son dialogue. This fathers' world was governed by the uncompromising logic of *That is the way things are, and no other way* – it was the only approach they understood and considered right.

But then suddenly, in Lérida, José and Juan had discovered theories that were the exact opposite of this unshakeable patriarchal world, which until then they had thought was the only one possible. They learned that things could be knocked sideways, unravelled, obliterated. You could refuse prevailing views without the world collapsing. You could say no to the prigs, to the arrogant, to the tyrannical, the servile and the cowardly. All could be swept away, for fuck's sake, the whole lot, all that wretchedness they loathed.

Their natural yearning for life was sucked into this great, stormy wave of hope as it knocked down everything in its path.

They let themselves be carried away by its tide.

They dreamed of mutiny, flamboyance, boldness, immense, unknown things that would spread beyond their lives and mark History. They believed in a full-blown revolution of hearts and minds.

They believed in such magic.

They said they now knew how to put their courage to good use.

They said they would no longer leave their wishes and desires behind, like an umbrella in a corridor, like *un paraguas en un pasillo*. Their fathers should bloody well get that into their thick skulls. The days of fear and self-effacement were over.

WE WANT TO LIVE!
¡QUEREMOS VIVIR!

A large crowd had gathered in the main room of the town hall. There were even more people there than during the festivities for Holy Week. Nearly all the men of the village had left the fields early, and some, in honour of the first day of the revolution, had put on their Sunday best. Several farmers in the room, like José's father, owned small plots of land, but most rented their land from don Jaime Burgos, and he employed the poorest among them as day labourers.

José and Juan barged their way through the crowd, *excuse me, con permiso*, and clambered onto the stage.

José stepped forward to speak.

He had never done anything like this before in his life.

He spouted great biblical sentences, like the ones he'd heard in Lérida, and the ones he'd read in *Solidaridad Obrera*. He said, *Let's be brothers, let's share our bread, let's share our resources, let's create a commune.*

All were hooked by his words.

He was theatrical. Wildly romantic. A dark angel fallen from the sky.

He said, *We no longer want to do all the whoring for the land-owners: they're keeping us in poverty and pocketing our money. We have a strength they can't even begin to imagine. The time has come to get organised. We can live differently. It's possible. It's become possible. We can live without anyone walking all over us, without any-one spitting on us, without anyone saying "You seem quite humble", in order to screw us over and crush us even more* (my mother: I got goosebumps at that point). *We will not be satisfied with a few crumbs, a few pats on the back. Our hardships have to end. The revolution will wash everything away. Our sensitivity, our feelings, will change too. We're going to stop behaving like children. We will no longer blindly accept everything they hurl at us.*

(Thunderous applause.)

In May, we travelled to Lérida, to work for some rich bastards, and let me tell you those cabrones felt the heat of our revolución (laughter). *We turned the place upside down, we said fuck you to the*

48

exploiters and we founded a free commune. We can do the same thing here. What's stopping us?

The farmers were transfixed.

José ramped up his attack. *They're taking what is yours by right, what you've earned through your hard work. It's unfair. Everyone knows it's unfair.*

(Applause.)

Is it right that a man should work like a beast for a few pesetas? Can we not create another kind of life for ourselves? Can we not abandon this constant competition that makes us wish our olives were bigger than our neighbour's?

(Bursts of laughter throughout the room.)

Momentous times, momentous methods, José said, copying the phrases he'd heard in Lérida. *Let's take back the land stolen from us, let's collectivise it, share it.*

(Thunderous applause again.)

A farmer raised his hand and asked with mock naivety:

And what about the collectivisation of women?

(Fresh bursts of laughter.)

A feeling of great happiness spread through the room.

Only the band of small landowners, made up of José's father and a few of his friends, and the group made up of Diego and two of his Communist comrades, did not seem to be sharing the general euphoria. Diego had a smirk on his face, as if he could already taste the forthcoming failures, before anyone else.

He decided to take the floor.

He said he was speaking on behalf of those who lived in *the* real world, in a real country, *y non en las nubes*, not in the clouds.

He said the decision to collectivise the land was too hasty, it could have dangerous consequences.

He said, *Let's just slow down. Let's be careful. We need to maintain a semblance of public order. Let's be realistic. We must wait.*

But the redness of his hair, the paleness of his skin, his frail shoulders and the coldness of his words lacked all appeal. Hardly anyone listened to him.

Why doesn't the little fucker mind his own business? José muttered to himself, and before he'd had time to think his reasoning through, he took to the floor again. He suggested not only confiscating land from the richest members of the community, but burning the land register and all the title deeds on a great big pyre. *Who's up for that?*

Arms shot up everywhere.

Motion passed.

The title deeds shall be burned in the church square on the twenty-seventh of this month.

The villagers applauded, celebrated and congratulated each other. Those who had been the quietest before became the most excited. Those least favourable to José's ideas – but who had quickly understood which way the wind was turning – changed their tune on the spot and started talking more animatedly than everyone else.

What we must still discuss, José said by way of conclusion, when things calmed down, *is whether the land should be shared* out in equal lots or according to the number of mouths to be fed?

A new meeting was set, in six days' time, to agree on the issue.

The village was in a state of effervescence the next day, at boiling point. Red-and-black scarves hung from windows and balconies, people basked in their newly acquired slogans, babbling away, gesticulating, panting, throwing themselves on the few copies of *Solidaridad Obrera* that had finally reached the village. They slaked their thirst for lyricism with torrents of sentences: *La gran epopeya del proletariado ibérico. The great epic of the Iberian proletariat. The triumphant march of the people's soldiers, the heartbeat of History in everyone's chests, the magnificent union of comrades in arms, sublime and filled with hope . . .*

Two days later, however, the general enthusiasm had somewhat subsided. The villagers had calmed down. They now mulled over the unthinking, puerile overexcitement of the previous days. Though no-one dared declare themselves outrightly hostile to José's proposals, a silent, barely acknowledged resistance began to take shape.

The most fractious of them all, the cobbler Macario, aired his regrets while playing dominoes (Double -six!). Decisions had been made in such a rush. *They were too hasty, too premature.*

Diego, don Jaime's heir, was standing at the bar. He agreed.

Oh, our resident carrot-top has something to say, does he? He speaks? the hairdresser said with a wink, addressing the room. *Well, I never. What has the Burgos boy got to say for himself?*

The Burgos boy, Diego replied, unruffled, *says we should keep calm. Imposing collectivisation on everyone is utter bullshit, and by playing the Anarchist heroes we're going to screw everything up. It'll deprive us of Europe's support at a time when they're shit-scared of the revolution.*

Because you think Europe is going to help us, do you? Why would they do that? Manuel said. *For our pretty eyes?* He was a C.N.T. follower, one of José's gang. *You think people in Europe are stupid enough to get their arses shot to pieces for our sweet faces?*

All I'm saying, Diego went on coldly, *is that there's no point scaring them even more with Bakunin-style, Anarchist drivel. There's no sense in that.*

The boy's got a point, Macario said. *He's not thick, despite his age.*

On the third day, sobered up and aggrieved at having given in to their excitement, the local farmers started to express their doubts and their burgeoning fears. Tempers and words flared at Bendición's café – to the point where the men sitting in front of their lined-up dominoes could scarcely concentrate on their game. Rants turned to bickering (*Hurry up and shuffle the tiles!*), appeals were interspersed with outbreaks of obscenity and nervous speculation (*Set the tiles!*), then came orations worthy of Socrates, flights of poetical fancy Cervantes would have been proud of (*Double-four!*), not to mention angry asides against the ruthless exploiters, attenuating circumstances to be considered (*It's your turn!*), uneasy shrugs (*Why's he taking so long? Is he fiddling with himself or what?*), then suggestions and rebuttals, all flowing one into another – the entire jumble punctuated by *coño*, blurted out every two sentences, and, to ram every comment home, *You motherfucker, me cago en tu puta madre*, often reduced to a succinct and efficient *Me cago en*.

Two principal developments emerged from these tumultuous café disputations:

    (1) Those who had been feverishly in favour of the decisions in the town hall were now feverishly worried about their consequences;

    (2) The number of people opposed to collectivisation had grown exponentially. From ten to thirty in a single day.

On the fourth day, those previously the quietest in the village had become more assertive, emboldened by the tension in the air.

All of them, or nearly all of them, insisted on order, discipline, for God's sake, please.

They were, of course, in favour of the revolution, who could doubt them? But they didn't trust the shit-stirrers importing woolly ideas cooked up by a bunch of perverted Russians.

The hooligans running amok in Spain's cities had fallen for these ideas first.

And José had mixed with them in Lérida – *no surprise there*.

The boy was driving his poor father mad.

He was a strange one.

An oddball.

He believed in universal happiness.

What a lunatic idea!

He really believed that men in these new great communes of his would become respectable, loyal, honest, generous, intelligent, grateful, courageous, kind to each other . . .

Pull the other one! (Laughter.)

That all conflicts would miraculously resolve themselves.

Qué aburrimiento! What a bore! (Laughter.)

That people wouldn't give a shit about their problems anymore, and every day would be like Sunday.

Oh no! Please! What? Lying around getting bored seven days a week, waiting to die?

That the dead would rise again (laughter) and thousands of other similarly extraordinary feats (laughter).

And José and his lot fervently believed in divorce.

¡Madre mía!

And polygamy.

Poly-what?

The right to screw ten whores at a time.

Is that all?

That these enchanted communes, where free love reigned between human beings, as pure as the morning dew, were little more than fantasies for sex maniacs with nothing in their brains and fire in their loins (the question of sex came back again and again – it troubled everyone, a lot).

Talking of arses and José, he's a bit special, isn't he? Un tío especial. He doesn't have a novia: weird, no? Is he queer?

A hundred reasons were put forth, from the most specious to the most absurd, with the sole aim of reneging on previous promises. Then came the crowning argument: *Who would be stupid enough to think we could get by without a boss with big balls to stop us from killing one another? Especially as we won't have money or power to set us apart?*

This open mistrust of José's ideas bound everyone together, just as the very idea of revolution had bound everyone together a few days earlier.

So, on the fourth day, fears once half spoken were being publicly expressed.

On the fifth, all but a few had recanted.

On the sixth day, the day of the second meeting, the town hall was packed. It was time to ratify the recantation.

For the first time, and to the astonishment of many, the women invited themselves along: a few were seething with anger, others were attracted by the prospect of a public showdown, most were merely worried their husband would fall for even wilder dreams. The poorest, the worst-off, the unhappiest, just came to say one thing: ¡Basta! Enough!

José and Montse's father stepped up first and attempted to voice his disapproval of the decisions made earlier in the week, at the risk, he said, chortling away, *of being shot by his own son* (giggles from the assembled villagers). He told them he'd slaved away his entire life to get something from his land, that his land was the apple of his eye, and it seemed only reasonable to him to wait for the war to be won before making decisions which weren't, *let's say, so very extreme* (mutterings of approval).

Diego stood up.

He spoke in blunt, brusque phrases, with all the seriousness of a government minister. He wanted to prove he had what it took. He wanted to show he was a man with a solid pair of *huevos* swinging between his legs. Tough words spouted from his mouth. He controlled his emotions. His measured arguments set him apart from the village hotheads with their red-and-black scarves.

He didn't approve of popularity-boosting projects and revolutionary fairy tales, *all the usual romantic-pubescent blah blah blah* (an expression garnered from *El Mundo Obrero*, the storehouse for his ideas). Nor was he in favour of *great big pompous sentences*, these were nothing more than an Anarchist show, *a trap for the unwary, a game of smoke and mirrors* (another expression from *El Mundo Obrero*), and designed to trick the naive – *it was like dangling shimmering lies at the end of a stick* (again from *El Mundo Obrero*). *All these preposterous promises were doomed to be postponed repeatedly by those who liked to peddle illusions.* They had to be avoided like the plague.

Furthermore, *all this waffle*, Diego said, as well as being totally unconnected to the realities of the village, *risked dragging it towards a desmadre* (meaning pandemonium, chaos and excess, an untranslatable word that had a big impact on the farmers in the audience). It was time to say *enough was enough. All this adventurous nonsense only flattered vain hopes; it would invariably end badly.*

Por un provecho mil daños. For one pleasure, a thousand pains, he said with an impressive note of gravity, and a dash of sang-froid.

Now here was someone who seemed reasonable.

The farmers nodded in agreement.

Diego intended to put the needs of the people first (*He must have sounded like our politicians nowadays? I say to my mother. They're all the same,* she replies, *crooks the lot of them*). *Everyone had to keep their feet firmly on the ground,* Diego said, *everyone had to be realistic.* The word "realistic" also made a strong impression on the crowd. *The villagers needed to cure their craving for unworkable ideals, show some political maturity, for heaven's sake.*

This is just scaredy-cat bullshit, José said to himself, bubbling with rage.

Diego had, of course, observed the regrettable disorder in the village in recent days, *a kind of havoc, if truth be told.* But instead of adding to this shambles (*Fucking hell, I'll smash his face in,* José growled), he wanted to try and remedy it. *Order. Rigour. Discipline. Without these, nothing was possible.*

(Warm applause.)

Furious and unsettled by this about-turn, José decided to take matters into his own hands. He did his best to hide his nervousness and control the wild beating of his heart. He used majestic words: "Justice", "Commune", "Freedom", the sort of words that mesmerise people in the first days of an uprising, but which quickly lose their power through overuse. And that's exactly what happened. José's words no longer aroused the same passion. He had shone in days past with his eloquence, but now it was Diego's turn to impress with his unexpectedly solid common sense. *Time does as it pleases*, my mother says, sounding, as she often does now, like an advertising executive. *What is nectar one day is poison the next, you've just got to get used to it.*

Diego seemed even more appealing to the farmers as he'd just said something infinitely reasonable: *Those who wished to collectivise should do so, and those who preferred to carry on as before should do so.* Why wouldn't everyone be pleased with that? It was called political sense. *Any blanket collectivisation would be dangerous*, he said. *Premature, perilous even. As for burning property title deeds, it would be wise to defer such a decision.*

But why wait? José shouted impatiently.

The war must be won before attempting a revolution, Diego said. *Any other decision would be irresponsible and threaten the village's stability.*

Now there was a man who knew how to speak.

Almost all the farmers were in agreement.

The meeting ended with a decision, approved by a majority: from now on Diego would make the necessary arrangements so that all the points agreed on that day could be implemented and complied with – and to reassure the local population, at a time of such great uncertainty, he would set up his headquarters in the town hall. After the troubles of the previous week, he would ensure that law and order were upheld and repress any activities contravening the decrees adopted by the majority.

This was Diego's big moment. His revenge. He was finally tasting the glory of the plan he'd been secretly hatching for months, years even: namely to show José and his friends a thing or two, and the bird-brained women who nudged each other whenever they saw him, and the village bumpkins who had kept him out of the picture for twelve long years whispering that he was a *zorro*, a little red fox, cunning as a *zorro*, mean as a *zorro*, phoney as a *zorro*.

Tomorrow is another day, José said, deflated, his pride wounded.

That day, as José headed home, distraught at the way events had unfolded in the village, Bernanos spotted a truck driving past him on the main avenue in Palma. It was filled with prisoners with disconsolate faces, yet they were scarcely noticed by the other passers-by. Bernanos felt as if he had been punched in the chest, but there was no sign of resistance, no protest from the people around him, not the slightest evidence of pity.

Bernanos could no longer ignore what his Catholic pride was refusing to concede. It was now as clear as day: in remote hamlets and villages, men were being rounded up every night as they came home from the fields. These men had not killed or harmed anyone, but they died with admirable dignity and courage. They were honourable farmers, he said, similar to the ones he had known as a child. Farmers who had obtained their republic through democratic means and who were happy for it, they had committed no other crime.

The slaughter now has a familiar routine: a farmer is on his way home, a bag containing a gourd of water and a last hunk of bread slung over his shoulder. Dusk is falling and the air is clear on the village road. He is tired, hungry, eager to get home and sit down. He has been tending almond trees all day for don Fernando, the big landowner who employs him for the season. The farmer's wife has laid out some plates on the table with bread, wine and a bowl of warm soup. She lights the oil lamp and sits down to wait, her husband's presence comforts her when night closes in and the shadows grow long. She hears her husband approaching the door. She would recognise that familiar sound among thousands of other footsteps. Yet before the farmer is able to take his place at the table, a gang of militiamen (some barely sixteen years old) burst through the door and haul him onto the back of a truck. It is the journey of no return. The last *paseo* (the last walk, as they call it).

Often the militia operate in the dead of night. They bang on a suspect's door with the butt of their rifles, or force the lock. They rush into darkened kitchens, turn chests of drawers upside down, kick their way into bedrooms and order barely woken men to follow them outside for a security check. Trying as best he can to get dressed, the victim is yanked towards the door, his braces hanging loose, before being wrenched from the arms of his crying wife. *Tell the children I* . . . Rifle butt rammed into his lower back, he is then shoved onto a truck where other men sit, silent, heads bowed, hands flat on their twill trousers. The truck sets off with a jolt. A few seconds of hope. Then the vehicle leaves the main road and rumbles down a dirt track. The men are ordered out, lined up and shot.

"Month after month," Bernanos wrote, "squads of killers, were transported from one village to another by trucks which had been requisitioned for one purpose alone: to murder thousands of so-called suspects in cold blood." The bastard Archbishop of Palma – who knew of these killings like everyone else – did not let it stop him from appearing in public, at the first available opportunity, "alongside the executioners, not a few of whom famously had the hurried deaths of a hundred men on their hands."

As if it were the most normal thing in the world, priests distributed to their congregations printed images of the Holy Cross framed by rows of artillery. (My mother still has one in her box of photographs.)

As if it were the most normal thing in the world, Carlist royalists sewed the Sacred Heart of Jesus to their shirts and executed men in the name of Christ the King, simply because a word they uttered had turned them into suspects.

As if it were the most normal thing in the world, the Spanish bishopric, in cahoots with the murderers, blessed the newly established reign of terror *in nomine Domini*.

As if it were the most normal thing in the world, all of Catholic Europe turned a blind eye.

In the face of such appalling hypocrisy, Bernanos could feel nothing but disgust.

I feel just the same all these years later.

*

José emerged from the village meeting a little disoriented, momentarily deprived of his ability to act.

Very quickly, however, as he walked down the steep calle del Sepulcro, with Juan at his side, he began to pull himself together.

He had supposed – *What an idiot I've been!* – that his dazzling ideas could win the day. He had reckoned any wavering or hesitation could be overcome. He had thought – *What an absolute fool I've been!* – that *to be* meant more than *to have* (he had recently come across a long article in the newspaper on the conceptual differences of *to be* and *to have* and it had impressed him enormously). He had just not fully appreciated – *This really gets me down!* – how the village bumpkins were actually more worried about losing their shitty goats and their crappy hovels than anything else.

And don't forget, Juan added, *as it's so important to them, their future plot in the cemetery.*

They're more worried about losing all that than smelling the sweet red roses of the revolution (sad, mocking laughter).

This was José's first lesson. He was bitterly disappointed.

He had to accept that anything that might lead to an opening up of the mind was taken for an abyss by the villagers. *They want flatness, dreariness, a changeless life.* It really threw him.

Juan – a bit of a pedant at the best of times – attempted to interpret the village's paralysis. José, absorbed in his own disappointment, only half listened. *I regret to have to tell you, my dear friend, not only do the locals here abide by the immutability of life, they cherish it, they cherish it just as they cherish the immutability of the cycle of the seasons, and the immutability of their olive trees on their immutable hills, just as they cherish the immutability of the ties binding them to the Burgos family and therefore continue to bend over backwards for them with immutable loyalty.*

Above all, they cherish their prejudices, José said.

In fact, Juan said, in an unusually loquacious mood, as he knew that spewing out sentences would help calm him down, *they hate novelty of any kind, however favourable it might be, as it feels like a sin, a transgression of the immutable order that rules their lives* (and then, feigning a professorial tone), *and of course they're right, it's a serious breach of the law of the preservation of energy which stipulates that the total energy of a system must remain unchanged over the course of time.*

Good luck explaining it scientifically, José said, with a rueful smile.

You could say they're rotting away in their own misery while imagining they're full of common sense. They're stuck in their old routines, only occasionally brightening them up with a few platitudes and four or five proverbs of earnest stupidity.

A bird in the hand, José muttered in a deliberately silly voice, *is worth two in the bush.*

Furthermore, you might wonder, my friend, Juan said, *why the 1934 revolt in Asturias didn't generate the same kind of enthusiasm here as it did elsewhere? It's because – and this is my personal theory, of course – the general enthusiasm that greeted the proclamation of the Republic simply fuelled the conviction here that the new order would change nothing in their lives. Besides, they don't give a shit about owning American goods one day.*

But that's not what we're offering them at all, José said, and he started to walk ahead, even faster than before, spurred on by his anger.

The two friends passed the grand house of the Burgos family, and José's anger turned to Diego – *the bourgeois son of a bitch has twisted everyone round his little finger.*

The ginger bastard is going to screw it all up. He's going to bugger the whole thing up, the shit-head.

Did you see how he lulled them all into a gentle sleep? How he sang a little lullaby to them with his "Be careful. Slow down. Let's calm down. There's no harm in waiting"? All that bloody fake wisdom. What a load of crap.

Serves them right though. What a bunch of fucking cretins.

Well, they certainly fell for it outright, suckers.

What a bunch of morons.

No better than mules!

Don't be rude about mules, por favor.

In politics, as in life, all they understand is the crack of a whip.

They'll get what they want with the redhead, then.

They can fuck off.

It makes me sick.

Those bastards can go and get screwed for all I care.

We have to get out of this shit-hole.

It was at that moment that José began to hatch a plan to leave the village.

He told his friend about the idea that had just popped into his mind: they were going to leave for the big city in Juan's father's truck. They could stay for a few days in the Oviedos' apartment, where José's other sister, Francisca, worked as a maid. Then they would join the Durruti column to capture Zaragoza back from the bastard Nationalists.

In her last letter, which Montse had read out to her parents (they didn't know how to read or write), Francisca had explained, with a certain degree of pride, that her masters, her *dueños*, had fled the city, leaving her with the keys to their apartment – such was their trust in her. Señor had a biscuit factory, while señora had a ridiculously long name and was descended from an uninterrupted line of extremely rich nobles. The Oviedos had been so frightened at the prospect of revolution that, after concealing the family jewels under the floorboards, and making a few money transfers to Switzerland, they had fled, fingers and wrists weighed down by gold rings and watches, to take refuge with señora Oviedo's family in Burgos, which had since fallen into the hands of the Francoists.

Events proved how wise the Oviedos had been to put their trust in Francisca. On the first days of rioting, when the militia were breaking into bourgeois apartments and chucking precious objects out of the windows, under the *guardia civil*'s untroubled gaze, Francisca's steady nerve had protected the property from any plundering or violence.

Barring the door to the apartment, Francisca had declared, head held high and hands on hips, that the militia would have to walk over her dead body rather than oblige her to betray her masters' confidence. They had always been good to her. There was nothing remotely Fascist about them apart from their wealth. Francisca's resoluteness had so impressed the four militiamen that they had abandoned the idea of bashing the door down, despite their burning desire to smash the apartment to pieces. *Now get the hell out of here*, Francisca shouted as they headed down the stairs.

What do you think of that, eh? (my mother asks me).

Pretty impressive.

On July 29, José told Montse he had decided to leave home. His ingenuousness, which had led him to believe that his village could become a free commune, was now directed towards hoping that the big city, with its more educated and more politically enlightened inhabitants, all well versed in the art of collective decision-making, would embrace the Anarchist ideas that were setting his soul on fire.

He was suffocating in the village.

Too many resentments, jealousies and fears were jostling for space under the guise of politics.

He wanted to meet people other than the usual crowd of witless farmers and their goats. He wanted to meet women too, for fuck's sake. He wanted to take to the barricades! It was time to be in the city. It was all happening there. His village filled him with horror: his mother's religious knick-knacks, the rosary wrapped round her wrist; the chickens pecking around in their own shit; his father's despotism and Aragonese stubbornness; the village parents speculating on their daughters' marriage prospects the moment a man brushed past them; and the frigid bitches of the village who wanted to remain virgins at all costs, to the point where you had no choice but to ask a donkey for kind assistance in getting your cock sucked (*What?!* Montse giggled with disbelief. *A donkey! That's absolutely disgusting*) – all those frigid bitches filled him with horror.

The idea of living his entire life in the same place, going through the same motions as his father, knocking almonds from the trees with the same pole, picking olives from the same trees, getting pissed every Sunday at the same café, *even* (he shouted this as loud as he could) *screwing the same woman until he died.* All this depressed him.

But where are you going to live?

With Francisca.

Do you have any money?

I'm going to join the militia and hook up with the Zaragoza front and Durruti. Do you want to come?

José's offer filled Montse with pride; it was as if she had been instantly and officially elevated to the rank of revolutionary.

You have to understand, my mother says to me, *that in one week I had considerably increased my vocabulary: despotismo, dominación, capitalist treachery, bourgeois hipocresía, the proletariat cause, the people have been bled dry, the exploitation of man by man. I'd also learned the names Bakunin, Proudhon, the words to the song "Hijos del Pueblo", and the meanings of C.N.T., F.A.I.,*

P.O.U.M., P.C.E. It all sounds like Serge Gainsbourg, doesn't it? And I, who'd just been an unripe walnut up to that moment, if you see what I mean ... Why are you laughing? I really was an unripe walnut, I knew nothing, absolutely nothing. I'd been forbidden from going to Bendición's café by my father. I thought babies came out of your bottom, I didn't even know what kissing was. I hadn't ever seen two people kiss. There was no television to teach me such things. I didn't even know how you performed the "Act" (she means sex). I had no idea what the 69 position was, or what a blow job was, nothing. Well, I, in one week, I became a hotshot Anarchist ready to abandon my familia without a grain of regret and without pity for my mamá's poor heart, her poor bleeding corazón.

Montse accepted her brother's offer straight away. Then she had a moment's hesitation.

Has our father agreed to this?

José fell about laughing.

From this day on, no-one will be dependent on another's good-will, not even the goodwill of their fathers, mothers, no-one, nadie.

Even so, Montse wanted to warn her mother. She immediately started to groan, Oh Lord, Dios mío! You're going to mix with those savages? Shame on us! What have I done to the good Lord? and so on.

Of all oppressions on this earth, José mumbled, a mother's oppression is the worst, the most universal, the most insidious, the most efficient, the most despotic. The one that prepares you, slowly but surely, to bear all other burdens.

Will you be quiet? his mother snapped.

José gritted his teeth and complied. He was still very much under her thumb.

One warm morning in July, the 31st to be precise, Montse jumped onto the back of a truck and sat down next to Rosita, Juan's girlfriend, while José and Juan climbed into the front.

José set off without arrepentiment (my mother says in her usual half-French, half-Spanish mishmash. She means regret: *arrepentimiento). José had never thought of leading the village, he wasn't chasing after power, but the old peasants who believed he was the underdog were wrong about him too. As for Diego, now he had long teeth, les dents longues, as you say, he was very ambitious, and all he said and all he did seemed to serve only one aim, one precise goal, but José's heart was puro, and let me tell you, chérie, such a thing as a pure heart does exist, believe me. José was a real gentleman, a caballero, you could say. He knew how to give to others, how to regalar, how to régaler, is that a word in French too? Anyway, he gave himself over to his dream with all the energy of his youth, all of it, and his honesty too. He hurled himself forward like a mad horse with a plan, un cheval fou, who wanted nothing more than to gallop towards beautiful new pastures. Why are you laughing at me again? There were many like him at the time because of the circumstances of the époque, you see, and he made a stand, not out of self-interest or for any ulterior motive, I can say that without the tiniest shadow of a doubt, not even the smallest ombrage of a doubt.*

It was time to say goodbye. Mother – all dressed in black, as she had been since the death of her father seventeen years before

– kissed her children as if she would never see them again. *May the Lord bless you and keep you safe!*

She tried to slip a thin gold chain with a medallion of the Virgin Mary around José's neck, but he pushed her away, embarrassed in Juan's presence. *Be careful crossing the city roads*, Mother said to Montse. *Look after your sister*, she said to José. *Don't do anything silly, you girls*, she said to Rosita. Then she just stood there, waving, until the truck disappeared into the final fold of the valley, as if it had been sucked into a crevice, and she ran back to her kitchen in tears.

Montse had promised her mother she would send word as soon as she arrived in the city. She felt calm, happy and serene, as if it were some sort of holiday, and this despite the war preoccupying everyone. Yet seeing her mother's black silhouette shrink into the distance, until it became a tiny dot, Montse had a fleeting, sad thought: her father was going to blame her mother for having let them go. He was going to torment her endlessly with reproaches and quite a few slaps (*a very common thing at the time, ma chérie*), as his punches appeased his suffering and relaxed his exhausted body. Her mother was going to find herself alone with the husband she feared (*another very common thing at the time, ma chérie*), and neither José nor she were going to be there to intervene or stand in the way of the belt he used on his wife, and on his children too, indeed on anything that wearied and oppressed him and he wished to banish from his mind by a good thrashing.

The truck bumped and swayed down the road towards the big city. As they drove through villages they were met by shouts of joy and cries of *Long live the Republic! ¡Viva la Revolución! Long live Anarchy! ¡Viva la Libertad!*

That afternoon Montse's mother ran into doña Pura, who told her some terrible news: don Miguel, the priest, had fled in the night to avoid being disembowelled by the bloodthirsty Bolsheviks.

Sweet Mary! Montse's mother made the sign of the cross. *What is to become of us, dear Lord?*

It's a disaster, doña Pura said with a sigh. Her anxiety was now so severe she had developed stabbing pains in her chest (she pointed to a spot below her heart), *they're like injections, like blades of fire.*

You mean like stings? Montse's mother asked, because she sensed she had to say something (she was too absorbed in her thoughts, and had been all day, to come up with anything more appropriate, too busy with her sadness, holding back her tears).

More like stabbing cocks, my own mother chips in, decades later, squealing with laughter.

This last comment requires a bit of an explanation. Ever since my mother has been suffering from dementia, she seems to draw great pleasure from the obscenity of certain words, the very words she shunned for more than seventy years. This is, apparently, a frequent occurrence in people exhibiting her particular symptoms, especially those who had a strict education when young. Illness cracks open the heavy doors of self-censorship. I don't know if the doctor's interpretation is correct, but the fact is my mother definitely enjoys telling her grocer he's a *bastard*,

71

calling her daughters (Lunita and I) *tight-assed bitches* and describing her physiotherapist as a *slapper*, then there's her love of words such as *cunt*, *balls*, *putain* and *merde*, all of which she bandies about at the first opportunity. This is the same woman who has done her best, since arriving in France, to weed out her Spanish accent, to speak in a refined way, who has done her utmost to alter her appearance so as to fit in with what she imagined was the French way of being (and by dint of this over-conformity she has merely proved to everyone that she is still a foreigner). Yet in old age she has begun throwing convention to the wind, linguistics and all. In a sense she is the opposite of doña Pura – don Jaime's elder sister and Diego's aunt – who, with age, tightened her grip on convention and battened down the hatches, *in the name of the Father, and of the Son, and of the Holy Spirit.*

HAGIOGRAPHY OF DOÑA PURA, OTHERWISE KNOWN AS SANTA PURA

Fifty-year-old spinster doña Pura had managed to transfer the discomfort caused by the repression of her most intimate urges and impulses onto the various organs of her irreproachably chaste body. The list of her aches and pains was endless. One day it was her stomach grumbling (the radishes from lunch had got lodged in her gut), the next it was her head that throbbed (bleak thoughts about the Bolshevik debacle), the day after that she had shooting pains in the perineum and a rather unsightly swelling of the stomach (both requiring a salt-water enema to loosen the bowels).

Her body protested at the brutal strictures her soul placed on it, and her aches and pains, truth be told, grew steadily more violent as they came up against unanimous, selfish and blatantly cruel family indifference.

In fact, distressingly for doña Pura, her own brother, don Jaime, had banned her from moaning about her daily suffering, going so far as to label it imaginary, even though it was the product of her excessive sensitivity, as if she were missing a top layer of skin (*missing a top layer off her tits and arse, if you ask me*, my mother cackles). As for her nephew Diego, he maintained, with typically youthful intolerance, that doña Pura's countless afflictions were just another way to piss everyone off, to poison the family atmosphere which was *bastante podrida, toxic enough already*.

Racked with constant pain, doña Pura was dismayed by these unjust and pitiless reactions, and she found consolation in the secret certainty that she would receive a reward for her suffering in a future life with Jesus Christ and his regiment of pink angels. Doña Pura had, of course, been brought up by a devout mother, taught by the sisters of the Sacred Hearts of Jesus and Mary, and steeped in Catholicism from a very early age, but her boring school-day religious precepts had acquired a new and fanatical urgency with the revolutionary events of July.

With true eucharistic fervour, doña Pura had begun to champion the Holy War waged by Franco, her venerated *Caudillo*, her absolute Genius, her heavenly Saviour, the valiant Architect of the New Spain, the zealous patron of noble causes, namely:

(1) the fight against the heathen;

(2) the eradication of the gangrenous spread of democracy which was inextricably linked to two notorious murderers (the mere mention of their names triggered headaches and necessitated medicalised inhalations of all kinds): Banikun, Bakinoun, Bakunin, whatever he was called, a Russian devil who advocated the rape of the people and property, and a lunatic named Stalin. Both of these men had no aim other than to trample over the values of *Hispanidad*, the very *Spanishness* handed down to her by her ancestors, of which she was the legitimate, undefiled custodian. These eternal Spanish values rested on a pedestal upheld by: (a) Christian piety; (b) love of the motherland; (c) *machismo*, a very Spanish and widespread pride (*otherwise termed syndrome of the stiffest beard or biggest prick*, my mother adds), which, depending on the social milieu of a given Iberian male, was expressed through bouts of anger, or sessions of wife beating – though this was conveniently forgotten by doña Pura, the poor woman had enough torments to be getting on with.

Beside her two aforementioned monstrous nemeses, doña Pura had recently added a third: the Anarchist bandit Durruti. The only place he deserved to be was in jail. As for President Manuel Azaña of Spain, whose physical ugliness was but the outer expression of his inner depravity (the instant she saw his photograph in the newspaper she was overcome by choking fits), he struck her as a weak man, indecisive, easily influenced, who wanted nothing more than to introduce Soviet-style egalitarianism to the country. He actively encouraged the contemptible debasement of superior beings to the level of mediocre ones, and the unhappiness of all. As if sharing out the world's misfortune could in any way diminish it!

Doña Pura rattled off her prayers during Sunday Mass, listing the very virtues she systematically denied in her everyday life (love thy neighbour as thyself, and other feats of spiritual magnanimity). *But who is not like that?* I say in protest. *I'm not*, my mother says innocently. *Doña Pura positively trembled with hatred at the sight of the pack of village thieves and young reprobates who made up the C.N.T. group. José, of course, was their star. Have you understood, ma chérie?* my mother demands. *Doña Pura, with all that Catholic rigidity of hers and that resentment, was a Holy Woman who attended every Mass and whose heart bled at the prospect of part of Europe slipping into materialism. She devoted all her energy to the improvement of her soul through the suppression of earthly pleasures and sensual delights, all earthly pleasures and sensual voluptés, that is. Don't tell me that's a caricature? I'm telling you she was like that in real life, pour de vrai, she really was!*

Doña Pura had a look of outrage etched permanently on her face, even when she was calm. But for all her holiness, she only granted her Christ-like mercy to a few deserving souls, those whose Catholicism could be certified. Chiefly, this meant:

(1) Don Miguel, a publicly recognised redeemer, who was genuine in his faith. Until the tragic day of his escape from the village, doña Pura consigned her bundle of moral and physical torments to him along with a big fat envelope (*filled with other people's money, of course*, my mother says). It was her spiritual credit, an envelope to cover the costs of running the church, and, once a month, as she put it into the priest's podgy hands, he would whisper, in his syrupy voice, *God will pay you back*, though he never specified how that reward might materialise;

and then:

(2) A few female rosary fiddlers, too feeble to defend themselves – from doña Pura's charity. This included Montse's mother (*the unfortunate woman has enough on her plate with that son of hers*), and a dozen or so other devout women (although their piety could never be fully guaranteed, *the poor are a sly lot, after all*) for whom doña Pura collected justly deserved alms such as second-hand clothes. Montse knew all about this as she was often made to wear old dresses that had been gifted to her.

Doña Pura enjoyed alleviating the suffering of the destitute, but her charitable works provided for the most part an excellent distraction (a powerful diversion, I might say) from her alarming and innumerable ailments, as innumerable in their manifestations as in the organs they affected, though the organs of her urogenital system suffered the most.

Husbandless, without children or a job, doña Pura also led one further vital battle (again to detract her from her countless ailments), and this time it was to impose domestic order on her household. Ordering had a deeply cathartic effect: saucepans and their corresponding lids were stacked according to a rigorously strict system; silverware was submitted to a thorough inspection followed by a wipe with a vinegar-dampened cloth. If that wasn't enough, Doña Pura then engaged in heated discussions with her brother on the choice of wallpaper for the hallway, she wanted it the colour of blood and gold, like the national flag, highly symbolic, so Spanish – *and why not decorated with wooden rods, bundles of fasces, and a life-size portrait of Mussolini?* her brother added sarcastically – but she just shrugged indignantly. Basically, doña Pura had many ongoing missions and each one served to evacuate and purge her of her painfully suppressed libidinous impulses.

A new torment had recently tacked itself on to her endless list of troubles: her nephew's conversion to Karl Marx's poisonous and progressive theories. *The man's name alone said it all!* Doña Pura begged God to forgive her nephew's apostasy, and, as a general panacea, she lit candles in the privacy of her room, praying that the poor boy, on whom she had placed so many hopes, would soon find his path back to the light of the Holy Catholic Church, or at least away from the Communist darkness encircling him – although such straying was wholly forgivable, Almighty Lord, in a young man who had suffered such neglect in early childhood, raised as he was by heartless nobodies (with Communist leanings no doubt).

Doña Pura secretly hoped her nephew's repulsive allegiance to Moscow, and the Republican vermin in general, was just the adolescent whim of a fool dazzled by an accursed siren, and that this whim would in due course fade, dissolving itself in marriage, which, according to the sacred word of His Holiness the Pope, remained the best solution for bringing stray and deviant sheep back into the fold.

In truth, Diego's escapades titillated her too, as did the depravity of the Bolsheviks who had blown up the holy grotto of Lourdes in France – *what horror, the end of the world might as well be nigh. That's nonsense,* her brother said. *I read it in the newspaper,* she snapped back. *Then change newspaper.* This was what her brother regularly advised her, telling her to curb her hatreds and crazes. Luckily, the recent arrival of German planes in Spain's blue skies had soothed her anxious heart. The planes were extra proof, if any were needed, that the Good Lord was looking after her motherland, efficiently supported in his task by his guardian on earth, the valiant Francisco Franco Bahamonde, *Leader of Spain, Caudillo de España, by the grace of God.*

No-one in the village could pretend not to know of doña Pura's hatreds and political inclinations. It was a time-honoured tradition, however, not to trouble the members of the Burgos family, just as no-one altered the *jota* or queried the order of the saints' days. Don Jaime Burgos Obregón's household had a reputation for uprightness and integrity spanning centuries, and people treated them with respect. They even rather liked the family and chose to ignore doña Pura's steadfast support for the Nationalists and her equally steadfast love for Franco, the only man who had managed to drive her to temptation, the only one to have got her heart beating with blessed sensuality (an anomaly in an otherwise resolutely chaste life). The villagers chose to turn a blind eye to all this. Yes, they knew doña Pura was a Fascist pig, a hundred per cent Fascist, and they knew that in the loneliness of her room she sang the Falange anthem "Cara al Sol", but they were prepared to forgive the poor dear as she'd never been screwed by anyone and *the inside of her chocho was undoubtedly sequito como una nuez, as dry as a nut.*

Just as he was about to begin writing his book, to denounce the villainies of the Catholic Church, the very institution so adored by doña Pura, Bernanos was assailed by doubts. What had he to gain from such an enterprise? I, too, question what I am achieving by reviving this past. As another one of my admired writers, the Italian Carlo Emilio Gadda, wrote in the opening pages of his book on Mussolini's horrors: "What is the point of stirring up this hornet's nest of which the world has already grown tired?"

Bernanos knew full well his truths were going to be hard to swallow and that he would be blamed for them. Yet he took the plunge all the same, not to convince anyone, he said, even less to whip up a scandal, but so that he could look at himself in the mirror, and remain true to the child he had once been, the child who had always found injustice so hard to bear. He decided to write, also, because he had seen his own tearful son Yves rip up

79

his blue Falangist shirt after witnessing the murder of two poor devils, two decent peasant farmers from Palma. (Yves deserted the Falange and fled Spain.)

Bernanos went ahead with his task because the Church's scandalous whoring for the military dug deep into his conscience. He knew he would be made to pay a price for his accusations, but he understood that it would cost him more to remain silent. He could no longer bear the sight of priests, the hems of their surplices soaked in blood and mud, handing out the Eucharist to lost sheep even as they were herded together for slaughter.

The tenets of what Bernanos called his "basic catechism" meant he could only feel revulsion for these murders committed in the name of the Holy Nation and Religion, the work of a small group of fanatics locked into the twisted folly of their dogma.

So he summoned all his strength, tuned his conscience to the beat of his heart, and decided to write about the things that were making him shudder with horror and disgust. He spoke about the widespread suspicion cast over everyone, how the Church rewarded informers, how those who dared to think differently or believe differently were kidnapped in the dead of night and slain without any form of trial. In short, he described what he termed a "consubstantial religious fury", and with it "the darkest, most venomous parts of the human soul".

His writing, Bernanos declared, was based on publicly known truths, proven facts, undeniable events. They would leave a trace in History, a bloodstain not even a sea of holy water could wash away.

They were the worst insult to Christ.

A total disavowal of his teaching.

A degradation of the human spirit.

This is what Bernanos wrote. He had the courage to do so, and his former friends never forgave him. To them he had become a dangerous Anarchist.

He knew, of course, that similar crimes were being committed by the Republicans, and that countless priests had been murdered by the Reds in similarly atrocious circumstances. They, too, were paying the price for crimes committed by their superiors (the small fry always get it in the neck while the big guys slip away). Bernanos knew the "Bolshevik bishops", as the poet César Vallejo called them, were just as cynical and barbarous as their Catholic counterparts.

But the fact that the Reds were massacring priests was another reason to act. The innocent women and children of Spain needed protecting. Guided by the spirit of the New Testament and Jesus' own heart, Bernanos believed that if there were to be a shelter on earth, a place for forgiveness and love, then it had to be within the bosom of the Church.

The bishops and cardinals of Spain had busily betrayed their flocks for centuries, warping and disfiguring the message of Christ, ignoring the needs of the poor the better to support their own clique of "well-heeled rogues", of "*canailles dorées*". The Spanish Church had long been the Church of the rich, the powerful and titled, and this treacherous perversion came to a head in 1936 when priests, in league with Francoist murderers, held out their crucifixes for the "guilty poor", the wrong-minded and deviant, to kiss one last time before being dispatched to the afterlife, *ad patres*. To serve as an example for all.

Bernanos attacked this ignominy. He told Their Excellencies the bishops that he completely understood why the poor became Communists.

So what if his words seemed a little reckless.

So what if they were foolhardy.

They mattered more than denial (a suppressed evil only resurfaces later, more violently than before) or polite indifference, which hardens the heart and numbs the tongue. Words mattered more than silence (it led to appeasement in Munich and the invasion of Czechoslovakia; and it was to be the reaction to twenty-five years of Francoist repression in Spain).

Bernanos chose to speak out: the Spanish Church had lost every last remnant of honour by underwriting the Nationalists' terror campaign.

So, now you see who the Nationalists really were, do you understand, comprendes? my mother asks me out of the blue as I'm helping her into her green armchair by the window.

I feel as if I'm beginning to understand. I'm starting to see the weight of tragedy carried by the word "national", and how every time it has been bandied about in the past, regardless of the cause (*Ligue de la nation française, Révolution nationale,* National Union of the People, National Fascist Party, etc.) it has inevitably brought violence with it, in France and elsewhere. History is awash with appalling examples. It was Schopenhauer who declared pox and nationalism to be the two ills of his century, and that while the former was curable, the latter was not. Nietzsche phrased it a bit more subtly. He said commerce and industry, the exchange of letters and books, the interdependence of high culture, the growing ability to move from one place or country to another, were all leading to a weakening of nationhood in Europe, with the result that a mixed European race might one day be born. The few nationalists to survive, he added, would be fanatics who would have to stir up hatred and resentment to exist. Bernanos, too, was deeply suspicious of the word "nation", though his former friends revelled in it. "I am not a nationalist," he used to say, "because I like to know exactly who I am, and the word 'national', on its own, is incapable of defining me . . . There is already not enough in our vocabulary to define what is precious to a man, without turning this word into a sort of badge or soapbox for all."

Personally, I tend to think that the people nowadays who like to latch on to the word "nation", (in itself, perhaps neither a good nor bad word; it is possible to have patriotic tendencies without being a Fascist), and thrust it about like a banner, do so to mask their true aim of separating nationals from non-nationals. In other words they are creating a system that differentiates and categorises humans.

This, I suppose, is just another form of xenophobia, and the objective is to go on and discredit the non-nationals, to marginalise them, and finally to get rid of them like parasites. The nation, of course, despite its immense and motherly generosity cannot feed others at the expense of its own children.

À mon humble avis, In my humble opinion, my mother says (she has developed a real taste for these flowery turns of phrase as they make her feel she's mastered French. She particularly loves expressions such as *Si j'ose dire, If I may say, Si je ne m'abuse, If I'm not mistaken,* she finds them most distinguished; they even seem to curtail her propensity to blurt out obscenities), *in my humble opinion, those we named Nationalists in 1936 wanted to purge Spain of all people like my brother. It was that simple. Y nada más.*

Perhaps the time has come for a quick lesson.

HOW TO PURGE A NATION

I. SPEECHES TO ENCOURAGE PURGING

Here's an extract of a speech by General Queipo de Llano, the great purger of Seville. It was broadcast on the radio in July 1936: "This war is a war to the death. We have to fight our enemies until their total annihilation. Those who do not understand this are not loyal servants of the sacred cause of Spain." Then an extract from the newspaper *Arriba España* dated the same month: "*¡Camarada!* You have an obligation to hunt down any proponents of Judaism, Freemasonry, Marxism and Separatism. Destroy and burn their newspapers, their books, their magazines and propaganda. Companions! We must do this for God, for the Motherland! *¡Por Dios y por la Patria!*"

In order to accomplish the aforementioned commendable aims, and free the nation of its vermin, the loyal services of informers were required.

II. INFORMERS

God's will is revealed through informers. They hail from all strata of society: a significant proportion are priests; high-society ladies who bleat on about their love of others and carry images of the delicately bleeding Sacred Heart of Jesus in their corsets; wives of high-ranking officers who are great pals with Father so-and-so (himself a remarkable cleanser of consciences); bakers; goatherds; farmhands; hastily catechised simpletons; lazy slobs in need of exercise; paupers who can be easily persuaded to hook a gun to their belts and rescue the nation; small-time thugs and major-league reprobates wanting to purify their souls and restore their dignity by wearing the blue Falangist uniform; some good folk, too, along with the unsavoury characters; and a large number of plain ordinary people (neither particularly virtuous nor particularly bad, of honest mediocrity, as Nietzsche might have said, like us all really), people who occasionally go to confession to flush out their sins, who never miss Mass on Sunday or Saturday's football match, who have sweet wives, husbands and three nice kids. Basically, people who are not monsters, or like those habitually termed monsters, not dissimilar to the militants of a certain political party in France today . . . actually, no, I mustn't make any far-fetched comparisons. As Bernanos said, only circumstances are monstrous and people give in to them, or rather they adapt their small stock of ideas to a situation.

These patriotic informers – instruments of God's will, it must be stressed again – don't trouble themselves with pointless procedures. They are people of substance, who bloody well get what they want, for goodness' sake. They don't get bogged down by pointless qualms. They just write a letter to denounce those who have aroused their suspicions and end their missive with a silky-smooth greeting to the powers-that-be, weaving in a mention of how proud they are to serve the Nation, including, of course, heartfelt thanks and sincere regards to señora so-and-so who was kind enough to have given them such delicious pears a while ago (the husband is a Francoist who doesn't mess around). The National Purge Committees take care of the rest.

III. THE NATIONAL PURGE COMMITTEES are primarily made up of bullies intoxicated by their ability to terrify others with their blue Falangist shirts and red Carlist hats. Excited at the prospect of testing out their brutality, they roll up their sleeves patriotically and sharpen their knives, eager to rid Spain of any riff-raff who refuse to toe the line – and ensuring that any dissidents are taught a lesson in national grandeur along the way.

Comments: a wonderful *esprit de corps* binds these committees together, and they are granted special dispensations by the authorities. They are notably absolved of the Church's fifth commandment (*Thou shalt not kill*).

IV. NATIONAL PURGING METHODS

National purging requires meticulous organisation and rigour.

Any excess niceties, which risk delaying or complicating operations, should be avoided: verifying that innocent people are not mistaken for murderers, for example. Whatever next?

The purging teams or squads, often referred to as "God's punishers", should preferably operate at night to make full use of the element of surprise and to stir up a maximum level of fear.

Teams can, of course, also operate in broad daylight on the street, or when breaking into homes, if suspects have been appropriately denounced by people with unblemished consciences.

V. LISTS OF PEOPLE REQUIRING PURGING BY THE FRANCOISTS: A TEMPLATE FOR ALL GROUPS REQUIRING ELIMINATION BY THE NATION'S SAVIOURS

(1) Desecrators of the Holy Cross and known non-believers;

(2) Individuals who are slapdash or careless in their religious duties;

(3) Individuals who have strayed from the path of national salvation (*desafección al movimiento salvador*);

(4) Teachers trained by the *Institución Libre de Enseñanza* (a secular and free institute) as they are enemies of finance and capital, perverters of young consciences, mentors of atheism and anarchism, both calamities for the nation's moral rectitude;

(5) Individuals loyal to any political party or union hostile to the nation;

(6) Individuals suspected of (or rumoured to have been seen) raising their clenched fists in support of the revolution;

(7) Workers rumoured to be protesting about their starvation wages;

(8) Individuals rumoured to have applauded when Republican aeroplanes flew overhead;

(9) Hypocrites who praise Franco in public and rebuke him in private;

(10) Irresponsible poets, writers and artists who encourage the illiterate masses to rebel;

(11) Miscellaneous others.

VI. THE THREE MAIN PHASES OF PURGING TO BE CARRIED OUT BY FRANCOISTS: A TEMPLATE FOR PURGES OF ALL KINDS

(1) The phase of so-called domestic or home-based cleansing. A typical case study: in the middle of the night, having banged on a suspect's door, a man is ripped from his sleep while his panicked wife begs to know if her husband is being taken to prison. The killer, who is not yet twenty years old, says, *That's right.* The suspect is hauled onto a truck where he sees three of his anxious friends. The truck sets off, leaves the main road and rumbles down a dirt track. The men are ordered out and executed, each with a single shot to the head, their bodies are lined up at the side of a grassy bank where the grave-digger finds them the following morning. The Francoist mayor of the village, no fool, registers the deaths of so-and-so and so-and-so, as well as so-and-so and so-and-so. Cause of death: stroke;

(2) The phase of so-called prison cleansing is as follows: prisoners languishing in overcrowded cells are led, in groups, to a quiet and secluded spot and executed, in groups, before being buried in ditches, in groups. As this classic method might be deemed too visible by some, the next phase, or so-called terminal phase, should be used as often as possible instead;

(3) The so-called terminal phase is as follows: prisoners receive the welcome news of their imminent release one morning. They sign the necessary forms and retrieve their personal items: every administrative procedure is

respected to exempt the prison authorities of any responsibility. Freed two at a time, the prisoners are executed the moment they step outside the prison grounds, their bodies taken directly to the cemetery.

VII IMPROVEMENT OF METHODS

As it would be too lengthy to list all possible amendments to the methods listed, improvements are left up to the purgers' discretion.

VIII ADDENDUM

Military methods can also be applied to proselytising. All one need do is address the form supplied below to any potential churchgoer of suitable age to attend Easter Mass. The form can have the same effect as a gun going off, but without the sloppy aftermath. Non-believers swiftly embrace the Catholic faith.

On the front of an envelope:
- *Señor, señora . . .*
- *Resident at . . . [street and house number].*
- *Attended Easter Mass at the following church:*

On the back:
- *It is highly recommended that churchgoers should be present in their own parishes for Easter. Any person having attended Easter Mass in a parish other than their own should provide proof of the fact to their priest.*

A detachable strip is included below for this purpose:

....

....

To facilitate administration, please detach this strip and send it, duly completed, to your parish priest. It can also be placed in the nearby collection box.

....

I'm listening to my mother and reading *Les Grands Cimetières sous la lune* in which the above addendum is transcribed. In the last few months my time has been totally taken up by reading and listening.

Until now, I had never felt the urge to roll doglike (but in a literary sense) in my mother's memories of the Spanish Civil War nor even to read any books on the subject. Yet now I feel the time has come to drag these events out of the shadows, since I had confined them to a hidden corner of my mind, probably the better to dodge any questions they might raise. I must now examine these events, look at them closely. I've never been aware of a summons like this before. It's the first time it's happened in my career as a writer, but I feel I must study the Anarchist chapter of Spain, a brief interlude of freedom for my mother, a moment of enchantment, which, I believe, was never replicated elsewhere in Europe. I am all the more delighted to revive this interlude as it has long remained unknown. It was deliberately hidden by the Spanish Communists, by the French intellectuals who were close to the Communist Party, wilfully obscured by President Azaña, who hoped he would win the support of Western democracies by negating the Anarchist chapter's existence, and suppressed by Franco, who wanted to reduce the Civil War to a clash between Catholic Spain and Communist atheism. But I must also study the vileness stirred up by the Francoist nationalists, the filth Bernanos observed without flinching, the sort of stuff that appears when men become fanatics and commit the worst kind of abominations.

In order not to be led astray by Bernanos' own chronicling of events, and by my mother's meandering, impaired memories, I consulted several history books. I hope I have been able to reconstitute faithfully the sequence of events that led to war, the outbreak of which Bernanos witnessed in a state of horror, his heart in his mouth, while my mother was thrown into a state of unforgettable sunny joy, black flags fluttering in the sky above her.

The sequence of events was as follows:

(1) The Spanish people were disappointed with the young Republic's constant foot-dragging and its president's permanent indecision.

(2) A ferocious smear campaign was directed against the Republic by the unashamedly powerful Church, an institution that had its owns banks and businesses, each one more powerful than the next.

(3) The bishops, the military and the propertied classes

came together in a sleazy alliance so as best to defend their interests.

(4) This alliance despised the hasty reforms carried out by the government to institute secularism and civil marriage, and

(5) wished to counter these reforms in the name of the Father, and of the Son, and of the Holy Spirit.

(6) The richer classes raged at the creation of a progressive tax on income, while the big landowners raged about the threat of potential land confiscations. Both groups had a brutal aversion to Socialism and its incendiary egalitarianism. They were dismayed by the idea of the people taking up arms.

(7) Revolution had been long and ardently yearned for by the radical left since the violent repression of strikes in Asturias in 1934.

All these elements contributed to a splitting of the country into two camps (each side grabbing hold of History for its own benefit). On one side, a so-called popular front – made up of various left-wing elements who soon came to blows before actually ripping each other apart – and on the other, a so-called national front made up of an alliance of right-wing elements, from the most honourable to the most extreme (all of them deaf to the pleas of a people who had been bled dry by centuries of wretchedness), and who refused to accept the new republic despite it being legitimately elected by universal suffrage.

On March 31, 1934, in Rome, the monarchist Antonio Goicoechea, the Carlist Antonio Lizarza, and Lieutenant-General Barrera signed an agreement with Mussolini to secure weapons and funding to overthrow the Spanish Republic. Between 1934 and 1936, scores of young people received military training in Italy and weapons were stockpiled by dint of Italian munificence. By 1936, the tension between the two camps in Spain was so fraught that a general election was called.

The *Frente Popular* won and appointed the progressive Republican Manuel Azaña as head of the country. Yet the situation grew steadily more explosive because of a coming together of various factors: partisan hatreds grafted onto class hatreds; fruitless bickering stoked by each party; fanaticism and blinkered thinking in all its forms; trickery designed to foil public opinion; political discredit hurled at the Republic (which was incapable of carrying out the necessary reforms, notably land reforms). Grievances built up on top of these factors, particularly financial scandals which badly embarrassed politicians of both sides who were caught redhanded. (On the left, Alejandro Lerroux, leader of a coalition government from 1933 to 1935, was involved in various shady affairs. On the right, Joan March openly and publicly amassed riches through corruption and smuggling and was thrown into jail by the monarchy, but later, in suspiciously hasty circumstances, became the financier of Francoism.)

94

On July 17, the garrisons in Morocco and the Canary Islands rose up against the legally elected government. On July 19, General Franco became leader of the insurgents. He thought all appetite for resistance would evaporate within three days if he unleashed his soldiers. He grossly misjudged the response. Upon hearing of the coup, the trade unions called a general strike and demanded the government distribute arms to them. On the night of July 18, the government authorised the handing out of weapons and released soldiers from any obligation to obey the insurgent military leaders.

Swathes of the population rose up against Franco and his coup, quantities of people who were only just becoming aware of their strength. In a few days, and with a speed the Anarchists or the Socialists would never have been able to achieve on their own, half of Spain, including six main cities, fell into the hands of the revolutionaries. As the revolutionary militia battled it out with the so-called Nationalists (the latter carrying out what Bernanos termed a reign of terror in the areas they occupied), and while priests in favour of the old order and hostile to the Republic were subjected to acts of extreme violence, thousands of peasant farmers started to divide up big agricultural estates without waiting for any law to be passed.

It's important to note that at the end of the nineteenth and the beginning of the twentieth century, there was such enthusiasm for Anarchism that many governments voted in drastic measures to suppress it. Yet it was in Spain, the land of the visionary Don Quixote who dedicated his life to helping the weak and trouncing evil-doers, that Anarchism came into its own. For the duration of one whole summer in Spain the movement truly blossomed.

Indeed, from June 1936 onwards, many villages were metamorphosed into free, self-reliant communes, stripped of centralised control. They survived without a police force or a judicial system, without bosses, money, churches, bureaucracy or taxes, in an almost ideal state of harmony. I believe it was this unique experiment my uncle José, along with a few companions, tried to replicate in his village. It was this experiment that my mother, thanks to various twists of fate, some tragic, some glorious, had the incredible chance of living.

Montse, Rosita, José and Juan reached the Catalan capital on the first night of August. The Anarchist militia had taken over. They had never felt so exhilarated in their whole lives. *Unforgettable times, des heures inolvidables,* my mother says, *and my memory of them, of those days, will never be taken from me, never, never, never, nunca, nunca, nunca.*

The euphoria on the streets was tangible and they witnessed unmitigated happiness for the first and last time in their lives. The cafés swarmed with people, shops remained open, passersby wandered along, as if in a drunken stupor, but everything worked as usual. Some barricades remained, otherwise the only signs of the ongoing war were vandalised churches with plaster saints smashed over their front steps. They reached las Ramblas.

The atmosphere, ma chérie, was indescribable, it's impossible à décrire. How can I tell you what it was like? So that you can feel that sensation too, as I did, so that it hits you right there, in the heart, en plein coeur. I think you have to have lived it, to understand what we experienced, it was such a shock, I was stunned. It was a total aturdimiento, a bewilderment, a revelación for us to discover the city that month of August in 1936. There were brass bands blasting out military music, horse-drawn carriages, flags hanging out of windows. There were banners slung from one balcony to another declaring death to Fascism, giant portraits of the three great Russian prophets, and militiamen in the street swaggering around with girls dressed in trousers. Buses painted with black and red initials, and trucks filled with young people waving guns charged along, and the crowds cheered them, crowds buoyed by a collective feeling of sympathy, friendship and goodness. No-one in the world today can imagine such a thing, no-one, and orators bubbling with ideas, perched on wobbly chairs:¡Míralos camarada! ¡Van a la lucha, tremolando sobre sus cabezas el rojo pabellón! Look at them, comrades! They head off to fight, their red hats bobbing on their heads. ¡Que alegres van acaso la muerte les aguarda, pero ellos prosiguen su camino, sin temer a nada o nadie! How merrily they go, even though death awaits them, but they go on, fearing no-one, nothing! From loudspeakers we could hear the latest news from the battlefront, with stanzas from the "Internationale" sung over these updates, repeated and belted out simultaneously by passers-by who greeted each other kindly, spoke to each other kindly, embraced one another without restraint, because they had understood that nothing glorious or new would come of all this unless everyone gave of themselves fully, and it was as if all the imbecilic things humans normally invent to torment each other with had vanished into thin air, pfffft . . .

My mother tells me all this in her language – I mean in that French of hers, a form of the language only she knows how to handle, or rather how to cripple, and which I constantly try to repair.

Montse and her companions headed towards the barracks used by the Anarchists. Trucks, jeeps and a couple of armoured cars were parked in the forecourt. Through the smoky fug inside the building, they saw two men sitting in front of Remington typewriters, bashing the keys with revolutionary gusto, while a third person stuck black and white flags on a map of Spain on the wall. Young people darted in and out of the room, some asking for information, others how to enlist and obtain weapons, others to rejoice in the progress of the revolutionary forces reshaping the world, *from top to bottom, I'm telling you, te lo digo, change was on the march, ma chérie.*

A man with slicked-back hair, like the popular singers of the period, lifted Montse up in his arms and she shrieked with laughter. A cowboy-like militiaman, a gun looped through his belt, welcomed José with a shove and asked him where he was from. *What a coincidence! From the village of F.?* He was from the village of S.! Brotherly embraces ensued. Two slightly pretentious young women in trousers, with red varnish on their nails, offered everyone filter cigarettes. Montse was astonished to see that women who smoked weren't necessarily whores.

I was really silly back then when I think of it, really I was.

One of the two men typing away at the Remingtons pointed them to the next-door room marked ORGANISATION OF INSUBORDINATION. The sign threw them into a state of infantile hilarity.

In the next-door room they found a man sitting amid a jumble of weapons and military equipment requisitioned from a local arms factory. He welcomed them, triumphantly claiming it was only a matter of hours before Zaragoza was captured. He handed José and Juan a leather gun-belt each, along with some ammunition holders. Even if these accessories did nothing but decorate their hips, the friends seemed amazed by them.

They left.

The night was beautiful.

They were happy.

They were sure of the infallibility of their cause.

They knew they were on the verge of something huge.

The Italian who had lifted Montse up in his arms accompanied them to a luxury hotel the C.N.T. had commandeered to use as a soup kitchen. Banners adorned the facade, each one scrawled with premature and naive declarations of victory. Montse would never have been to such a palatial hotel had it not been for the war and, after three attempts to get through the revolving doors (*Oh dear, what a peasant I was in those days, I'm embarrassed to think of it now!*), she discovered the flabbergasting luxury of the place: chandeliers with crystal pendants, vast mirrors with rococo gilt frames, wooden tables with carved leaves and flowers, and elegant white china plates flecked with gold leaf.

I couldn't get over it, my mother says, *I was totally stomaquée, punched in the stomach, isn't that a word?*

It's *"estomaquée"*, I correct her.

Ah, is that right? With an "es"? I was estomaquée, then, by the richness of it all, so much wealth.

They dined on fresh sea bream and rice – the only fish Montse had ever eaten were the salted sardines from the drying barrels at Maruca's.

They found their way to a café on las Ramblas.

Pinch me.

Tell me I'm not dreaming.

Tell me it's not going to end.

These were the kind of sentences whizzing round Montse's head.

At the Aurora, a café newly collectivised like all the others in town, Montse remembers a sign over the counter warning that tips would be refused.

The days of degrading charity were over.

The waiter had removed his bowtie in honour of the revolution, but had kept his white apron and a clean cloth folded over his wrist. He zigzagged between the tables with torero-like grace.

For the first time in her life, Montse drank a *copita* of Anís del Mono. It burned her throat and tasted good. José and Juan laughed as she pulled faces.

This is the taste of life!

She heard foreign languages for the first time. They seemed to comfort her soul. The place was teeming with young people who had come from every corner of the world to support the Republican army: Americans who were twice her brother's size, Englishmen with milky white skin and rosy lips (*not very attractive lips*), Italians with gleaming hair, as well as Austrians, Frenchmen, Germans, Swiss, Russians, Hungarians, Swedes. *People spoke loudly – for some reason, who knows why, the Spanish always think everyone around them is deaf.* They smoked, they laughed, they addressed each other using the familiar *tu* even though they had never met. *In that jaleo, that din, in that brouhaha of voices – don't you love that word, ma chérie? Brouhaha: what a fantastic word for din, for babbling – anyway, in all that laughter, with the clinking glasses, and swearing hurled across the room, there was suddenly this deep and vibrating voice … Actually, Lidia, ma chérie, before we carry on, could you pour me a glass of anisette?*

What? Right now? At this hour of the day?

Please, my darling. Just a drop, une goutte, a tiny drop.

I look like I'm hesitating. My mother gets impatient: *I may well die tomorrow and you want to stop me drinking an anisette?*

I pour her a small glass of sweet aniseed and sit back down next to her.

So, suddenly, she says, setting off again, pretending she's shivering with intensity – *touch my arm, right there, touch it! – a young man is standing there, bolt upright, and he starts declaiming a poem. He's French, ma chérie. His poem is about the sea and nothing else, just the sea. He's as handsome as a god, with graceful hands, artist's clothes. I can see him now as clearly as I did back then. No-one says a thing. We're all listening. At the end of his poem everyone starts clapping.*

My mother slips into a momentary daydream, there in her green chair by the window overlooking the playground. I can't help but think of the babbling linguist of a poet, a regular on the literary circuit, whom I'd seen perform the night before, out of pure curiosity (that'll teach me), and who, after inflicting his poem on us all – something about a man having a front and a behind (not much drama there) – went on to tell us about the major risks he'd taken in writing the poem . . . oh well.

Anyway, in the café where Montse and the three others were seated, conversations gradually resumed after the poem, everyone soaking up the sort of short silence that follows a moment of pure artistry. Discussions got going on exalted subjects, alcohol fuelling exalted sentiments, and they progressively veered towards more colourful and earthy subjects (my mother chuckles at their memory).

Life is fun, I love all this, that's what I told myself, my mother says.

Conversations ranged across these subjects:

• Durruti, his magnetism, heroism, loyalty, and generosity, his integrity and his humility, too, which meant he slept on the same dirty mattresses as his fellow fighters and ate the same revolting rice – he was very different from the scaredy-cats who sent others to their deaths while sipping whisky on the rocks through a straw;

- the latest news from recently founded communes in the area;
- the dramatic developments on the Zaragoza front;
- free love and prostitution;
- the different contraceptive methods (how to choose between *coitus sodomiter*, *coitus onaniter* and *coitus condomiter*);
- the recipe for *cocido*, a patriotic dish if ever there was one, opinions differing on whether it should have sausage in it or not;
- then the different *garbanzos* which go into the dish, *you know, chickpeas – why they're called that, I just don't know,* the most exquisite, the most delectable, the most Spanish of foods, princes of the Fabaceae family, sources of energy, deliciously scented, well known for their upstanding, erectile properties when consumed by men, and which make them fart more than women – *Why? Who knows – a typically male Spanish joke,* my mother adds;
- the shocking lack of any poem dedicated to chickpeas. What have César Vallejo, Miguel Hernández, León Felipe or Pablo Neruda been up to? (*Neruda, that son of a bitch,* my mother adds. *What do you mean? I ask. I'll tell you later.*) What are those lazy poets waiting for? A poem to chickpeas!
- the difference between male and female farts, in terms of their musicality and fragrance, their curative and preventative functions, besides their ability to see off any enemy;

- fart-lovers and fart-haters, two distinct and irreconcilable categories, split by gender, even though the revolution was going to make up for this despicable discrepancy.

Young women, embrace modern times, from now on you can fart with revolutionary abandon! (laughter).

Maybe we could discuss more serious matters? a young Andalusian philosopher suggested (*actually he looked just like your nice friend Dominique*). *If we study this question of the inherent vulgarity of the Iberian people closely, and note their fondness for chickpeas, which naturally leads them to a tendency for flatulence, and then compare that to French vulgarity, which is more discreet and tempered by a love of haricot beans, it transpires that these differences are remarkably reflected in literature: Spanish literature loves to stress bawdiness, you only have to read* El Buscón *by Francisco Quevedo to realise this, while French writers of the same period come across as strait-laced teachers of catechism. French literature, after the establishment of a national academy in 1635, put paid to the sort of lewdness beloved by Rabelais, who wrote with such genius, because Rabelais, my friends, was actually Spanish in spirit, for sure, claro, a brother to Cervantes, his hermano, and what's more a free-thinker, if not an Anarchist. So, to Rabelais' health,* all those present shouted, *a la salud de Rabelais!* even though they knew absolutely nothing about this so-called genius (*anyone putting their head round the door would have thought we were all crazy,* my mother says).

And so, in a roundabout way, we came back to the genetic incom-

*patibility of Communists and Anarchists, and the arguing kicked off
again with new bursts of swearing, coño, joder, me cago, and other
obscenities echoing round the room.*

Montse listened to all these conversations.

It was as if her life were speeding up and the very basis of
its progression – from childhood to adulthood, and then from
old age to death – had somehow got caught up in itself and been
fast-forwarded at breakneck speed.

*It was as if my real life was just starting. A bit like when your
father died. When was that?*

Five years ago.

I can't believe it. Really? It feels like a century ago.

Do you think of him sometimes?

*No, never. I even wonder how I could have spent so many days
with him, so many nights, so many meals, birthdays, Christmases, so
many evenings in front of the television, and not remember a thing,
I've not the slightest memory of any of it, nothing.*

The four of them left the café.

Montse felt as if she had sprouted wings, as if a spell had
been cast over her.

There was a lightness to the air, an effervescence. It acceler-
ated everything, sweeping anxiety away.

I love life: that's what I thought back then, my mother says.

Montse returned to the bourgeois apartment her sister,
Francisca, looked after for señor and señora Oviedo.

The place dazzled her. She had lived in the greatest poverty
all her life, without even dreaming of the opulence enjoyed

by some. She had only ever caught sight of luxury the time she briefly visited the Burgos household (the day don Jaime declared, *She seems quite humble*).

In one evening Montse discovered (her creased, wrinkled face lights up with joy when she describes this) the existence of running water, hot and cold, bathtubs with wrought-iron tiger feet, lavatories with flushing mechanisms and flip-up lids, electricity in every room, refrigerators, clocks, thermometers on the walls, telephones made out of ebonite. In a few hours, she encountered the wonders of modern, fairy-tale-like comfort. She was amazed by the thick woollen carpets, the silver toast holders, the extravagant leather sofas, the framed portraits of moustachioed, mummified old men. Yet what seemed to her to be the absolute pinnacle of chic was a silver spoon with a right-angled handle to scoop up powdered sugar.

The lavishness of the place astounded her.

Just having a bath plunged her into ecstasy.

She didn't tire of opening the refrigerator, with its ice-cube drawer, and pouring chilled water into a cut-glass tumbler.

She screeched with pleasure at the sight of the green Formica table in the kitchen (like all those who have grown up in poverty she still prefers new things to the kind of old country furniture she used to see in her village). For the first time she ate butter at breakfast – what she still calls *veurre* in French rather than *beurre*. *I can never get "veurre" right, can I, darling?* my mother says. Nothing like the lard she used to have back in her village.

Veurre was a delicacy.

She was astounded by señora Oviedo's extensive collection of clothes. It filled an enormous wardrobe. *Guess how big the wardrobe was?* my mother asks me. *Six metres long!*

Wealth really is a blessing on earth, a consolation, a delight, Montse told herself when José wasn't there (he found the apartment's overabundance of luxury repugnant: counter-revolutionary, to be precise).

Nothing had prepared Montse for it, nothing she had learned from the nuns, nothing she had learned from her mother or her aunt Aparición (the aunt she called Pari). She could never have imagined being so overwhelmed by it all.

Montse had never, of course, seen anything beyond her home village. She'd never read romantic novels or anything to help explain love and sex to adolescent girls. She'd grown up in an immensely puritanical family, out in the sticks, utterly ignorant of the world. She was convinced it was a wife's duty to shut up. She was convinced all fathers had the power, by some sort of decree, to beat up their wives and children. She'd been brought up to fear God – and the Devil, who, *be warned, young lady*, can take on a thousand disguises. In essence, she'd been perfectly trained to obey and submit.

This meant that everything that happened to her in the big city overwhelmed her as powerfully and immediately as an earthquake.

Yet Montse was still able to slip into the new and unknown world of the city with genuine ease and happiness. It was as if she'd been born into it.

The air seemed lighter, relationships freer.

The everyday things she witnessed – the tiny instances that made up ordinary life, the hot water running from the taps, a cool beer on a café terrace – were all miracles to her.

It seemed life was becoming true, véridique. How can I explain that to you?

In *Works and Days* Hesiod wrote: "For the gods keep hidden from men the means of life." At the age of fifteen, Montse was discovering a life that had been kept from her. She pounced on it, and wrapped herself in it. It was a moment of pure joy. Seventy-five years later, however, it means she can, with typical Iberian theatricality, declare that the war still goes on even if the armed conflict was lost by her side.

Now, listen to me, escúchame!

I'm listening, maman.

You see, if you asked me to choose between the summer of 1936 and the seventy-five years I've lived since you and your sister were born, I'm not sure I'd choose the latter.

Oh, thank you, I say, a little put out.

At the beginning of her stay in the city, Montse worried about getting lost in the maze of streets and she rarely ventured out. She soon discovered the thrill of just strolling, pausing to admire the shop fronts with their lingerie displays of low-cut bras, lacy suspenders and pink silk slips which excited her wildest fantasies of love (tolerated by the revolutionaries even though contrary to the notion of women's emancipation).

She discovered the sea.

She was frightened to touch it.

She ended up dipping her toes in and letting out a cheerful squeal.

She walked round the city parks with Rosita and Francisca, listening to Anarchists giving impassioned speeches on wooden boxes, applauded by hundreds of bystanders. The girls stared at the men in the crowds. They dreamed of love. They invoked it, they spoke to it with nervous hope and sighs of all kinds. Of course, they were in love, merely missing an object for that love.

Montse distinctly remembers dawdling along a main boulevard with Rosita when an unusual gathering in front of the Banco Popular Español caught their eye. The two girls discovered four men standing around a fire while a fifth leaned forward to throw wads of banknotes into the flames. No-one seemed to want to grab the money, stop the man or voice their dismay at this blatant waste. Montse and Rosita were afraid they'd come across as uneducated peasant girls if they expressed their surprise. They had been brought up with the constant anxiety of having to save three *pesetas* here and there, of not wasting a crumb, repairing clothes until they finally fell apart. They had lived the most parsimonious lives, if not to say the most money-pinching. Their mothers had taught them a real yearning for thrift from a young age (thrift was more than just a concern or a priority, it was a strong and violent passion), but the girls considered the money-burning that day, however staggering, to be in the order of things – just like everything else that summer of 1936, the summer when all values were turned on their heads, when all behaviour ... *This is what I want you to understand, ma chérie ... everything was thrown into disarray, feelings were cast up into the sky, vers le ciel, that's what you have to get, that's just how it was.*

If I think of it now, my mother adds, *if I'd pinched one of those wads of notes I wouldn't be in the financial mess I'm in today.*

My mother has never had much opportunity to burn banknotes or light a cigarette with her spare cash. In order to feed and clothe us as children she had to stick to some rather strict rationing, resorting to the kind of frugality she'd learned from her own mother. She never trusted banks again after seeing those notes go up in smoke. She hid all her money under the carpet in her bedroom, stashing it away patiently for her old age, but over time the notes lost all value.

My mother: *I got them in the end, didn't I?*

Me: *Who's that?*

My mother: *The bankers, of course.*

I listen to my mother describe the money-burning episode, something I've never read about in any book, and which seems to me deeply emblematic of that period. I'm left wondering what else my mother has retained from that extraordinary summer – the thought haunts me. What has she held on to from those times which now seem so unthinkable, days when people burned wads of notes to show their disdain for money and the madness it brings? Does my mother have more than just memories from that period? Have her youthful dreams all but dissolved? Have they just disappeared inside her, settling like sediment at the bottom of a glass? Or is there still some flicker, a will-o'-the-wisp in the darkness of her old heart? It's what I sincerely hope. What I know, for sure, is that my mother doesn't give a damn about the little money she has left, and she willingly hands it out to people, left, right and centre. The doctor puts this largesse down to her illness, along with her memory loss and her repeated, or rather incessant, linguistic misdemeanours.

I'd like to think her doctor has got it wrong and that a remnant of light from her past dreams still glimmers inside her, that the embers of that month of August 1936, when money was burned like refuse, are still warm.

While Montse marvelled at the beauty of the world, José put off joining the militia for a few days. He spent his time in cafés, chatting with other young men like him about how the revolution was going to reshape the world. He began to feel uneasy. He couldn't help but detect in all the speeches and revolutionary propaganda – the city walls were plastered with the stuff – the same kind of simplistic, rote catechism the village priest used to employ. It was just as falsely optimistic and filled with similarly grandiloquent statements, designed to make dreamy young people swallow any old crap: "Courageous young chests are the best defence against the Fascist vermin. Follow the triumphant march of our gracious gladiators as they sow the seeds of a new generation of faithful servants with the favourable winds of our ideals behind them . . ." All the usual gibberish and bluff.

José realised he was just as guilty of spewing this nonsense as everybody else. They all wore these clichés and lofty proclamations the way others wore ties. This upset him, a lot.

But what troubled him the most, and he couldn't share this with anyone since he could scarcely admit it to himself, was that he feared that his joining the militia would change nothing at all.

José had never felt such a strong urge to give himself over to a cause, but, at the same time, he had never been so convinced that his peasant knowledge, his farmer's courage, would sadly serve no purpose and only lead to death. For the time being he wanted to live, for fuck's sake, he wanted to live. He wanted to smell coffee in the morning. He wanted to stare at the sky, at women, at the fountains, at the olive trees, at the long-suffering gentle donkeys of his village. He couldn't understand why so many young people were heading off to the battlefront, their chests and arses stuck out in that very Spanish way, ready and eager to be massacred.

José could see how those conducting the war on his side were making it up as they went along, with scant resources at their disposal, waiting for weapons to be supplied to them. They were painfully lacking in military know-how, quite incapable of reading an Ordnance Survey map, incapable of establishing any sort of fighting strategy, and, consequently, totally useless at getting men ready for battle. José had frequently heard them mock the army, joking about lanyards, stripes, medals, epaulettes and moustaches, and the other trinkets officers liked to decorate themselves with, deriding anything that remotely reminded them of life in the barracks and its distinctive stench of feet.

José knew this sarcastic disdain for military matters, this soft-headed trust in good intentions, probably meant slaughter for all the young people marching triumphantly off for the greater glory of the nation. He knew these good intentions would be met with shots from a Mauser K.98, and their officers' idealism would be cut down by sweeps of machine-gun fire – he had not yet heard of humanist homilies silencing a machine gun. These youthful Don Quixotes were heading off to battle with flimsy espadrilles on their feet and cotton rags on their backs. They knew nothing of the art of war, of its arbitrary insanity, of its heinousness and savagery. Lacking in training – proudly waving rusty guns they didn't know how to aim, or adjust the sights to, or even how to load the bullets, and carrying home-made grenades that could explode in their faces at any moment – these young volunteers, barely eighteen years old, were doomed to fail against an army as battle-hardened and powerful as the Nationalists.

And when these volunteers finally arrived at the front, under-nourished, poorly armed, stupefied by lack of sleep, numb with cold, what might have seemed abominable to them in any other circumstance, namely collective murder, would suddenly seem bearable. So when they'd lost their strength to string two thoughts together, when they were merely focusing on surviving and fighting, no longer asking themselves any questions, when they were just carrying out automatic gestures without any awareness of good or evil, without a trace of emotion left, they would simply fire their guns, on command, at other young men who seemed more methodical, with impeccable boots and impeccable uniforms, but who were just as deceived by the propaganda from their side, which had spun magnificent lies about their struggle, and promised them – in return for a posthumous medal or very often sod all – the eternal gratitude of the motherland. What a joke.

But precisely because José was of peasant stock, used to tilling and breaking the arid earth with his plough, he knew that the human spirit could not overcome matter, especially if that matter came in the form of an M.G.34 machine gun. He knew full well that you couldn't fight anyone with three stones and an ideal, however noble your cause, least of all an over-trained army with cannons, panzers, bomber aircraft, tanks, armoured vehicles, artillery of all sorts and machines designed specifically for the eradication of other humans.

As for the foreigners who had joined the Republican ranks, emblems of the international fight against Fascism, José watched them posing for photographers, holding their guns in the air, saluting with clenched fists, sunning themselves on café terraces, getting drunk on exaggerated words and feelings, chatting up the local *guapas* by whispering sweet nothings in their pretty ears. He realised their presence was sadly more symbolic than useful (at this point he remembered he had to keep an eye on his sister, as the first good-looking dandy to come along would be liable to seduce her and get her pregnant).

An unanticipated perplexity took root in José. Nonetheless,

he still hoped he could be part of the revolution and the war. He hoped as much, but small fissures had begun to dent his optimism.

He had desperately hoped to play a role in an uprising that changed the course of History, but now he wondered what the hell he was doing, watching trucks full of young people being driven off for slaughter. He listened to the Russian representatives with round-rimmed glasses warning the foreign volunteers of the cunning plots being concocted by the Anarchists. He witnessed interminable squabbles in the cafés between Communists and Anarchists, each side accusing the other, both guilty of their truths, one blinding and the other self-deceiving. Exactly the sort of parochial bickering he used to hear back in his village.

To add to his growing doubts as to the chances of a Republican victory, a new worry had taken hold of José: he had left his father to cope alone with the ploughing and harvesting. Just as an irrepressible urge had led him to flee his parents, he was now overcome by the urge to see them again. He remained attached to them in ways he found hard to decipher.

He had to go back to the village. His instinct told him he should. He weighed up the pros and cons for a couple more days, and then one particular event helped hasten his departure.

He was enjoying the cool evening air on the terrace of Café Aurora on las Ramblas, drinking a Manzanilla, watching people go by, vaguely listening in on the conversations around him.

At a nearby table, two men were knocking back glass after

glass of plum brandy. They spoke so loudly he couldn't help but hear them. They were in high spirits, grinning from ear to ear, and burped and congratulated each other. They seemed extremely pleased with themselves, with their bravery, and patted one another on the back. *They'd done fucking well, hadn't they?* Having sniffed out two priests who were quaking with fear in some cellar, they'd wiped the first one out with a blast of gunshot to the face and told the other one to peg it, and then they'd shot him in the back as he scampered away, *bang, bang.* *Two cassocked devil-dodgers bumped off in one day.* And they had been afraid they would have to go home empty-handed. *Not bad for a day's hunting. Bloody hell, you should have seen how those little pulpit thumpers shat themselves. Priceless.*

The two men thought they were very amusing.

They were surprised José didn't seem to share in their delight.

Was he a secret Francoist or what?

José wiped a hand across his forehead, like a sleeper awakening from a nightmare.

It was as if he'd been punched in the stomach – exactly what Bernanos was feeling at the same time in Majorca, and for the same reasons.

José remained glued to his chair, paralysed with dismay, more dead than alive.

So it was possible to kill human beings without their death giving rise to the smallest pang of regret, not even a tinge. Men could be exterminated like rats. Without remorse. It was actually something to boast about.

What sort of corruption had to take place, what sort of lunacy, in the name of a "just cause", for such horrors to be countenanced?

Don't kneel down in front of anyone. No os arrodilléis ante nadie. Don't betray yourselves.

What depths of abjection would these two murderers discover if they examined their consciences one day? José could no longer turn from the truth he'd carefully chosen to ignore as it was now screaming out to him in such a brutal way: every night, militiamen were setting off on punitive expeditions, murdering priests and purported Fascists. These crimes were possibly more widespread in Majorca, even though I've not been able to count them all, but the point is obviously not just the number of people murdered. José, just like Bernanos in Palma, had observed a hatred gnawing away at his comrades, a hatred that was condoned, encouraged, a hatred that was (as people might say today) uninhibited. It was not afraid to show itself, it was even proud.

José now only had one thing on his mind: he wanted to go home as quickly as possible. He'd decided. He wasn't going to enlist. He was perhaps going to be called a coward and a quitter, but he didn't give a damn. He was going home to the village, with Juan and Rosita. Montse could stay with Francisca since she was refusing to leave.

It would help her mature, grow up a bit.

He had no idea how right he'd be on that score.

117

The next day was August 8 – my mother remembers this without a moment's hesitation (Me: *You remember that date?* My mother: *According to that arse of a doctor, my head is all mush, but just look!*). It was the day the French Cabinet voted not to intervene in Spain, even though, of course, it regretted the hideous conflict destroying its beautiful neighbour to the south.

> *Españoles, que vivís el momento más trágico de nuestra*
>   *historia.*
> *¡Estáis solos!*
> *¡Solos!*
> People of Spain, you who are living the most tragic
>   moment of your history.
> You are alone!
> Alone!

The pleas of the writer José Bergamín (paradoxically a Catholic Republican, cultural attaché to the Spanish Embassy in Paris) for financial and moral support from the French government had come to nothing.

The war veteran associations in France had advised their government to stay neutral in all matters regarding Spain. Saint-John Perse, the petrified French poet and diplomat, went along with it.

As for the Soviet leaders, they continued to hesitate a little longer – meanwhile Hitler and Mussolini were helping the Francoist troops cross the Strait of Gibraltar.

Not until September did Stalin agree to back the Republicans, and only then did the first boats with military equipment set sail from Odessa.

No words are strong enough, my mother says, *to describe the disillusionment, the disappointment mixed with anger, mezclée de ire, that José experienced when he heard all this news. When I – what do you call it now? – reverse in my spirit, do a backward movement, a marche arrière, I mean go back in my mind, ma chérie, to that time, I realise it was then, if I'm not mistaken, that my brother's sadness started. It was right then, at that very moment.*

In Palma the months went by and the horrors only got worse. Bernanos found out that the Crusaders of Majorca, as he called the local Nationalists, had recently executed all the prisoners they had picked up in one night, having driven them "like cattle to a nearby beach where they were shot, in quick succession, one beast after another". Once the job was done, the crusaders placed "the cattle in a pile, absolved cattle heaped with unabsolved cattle", and sprinkled the lot with petrol.

"It's quite possible," Bernanos wrote, "that this purification by fire, thanks to the presence of serving priests, took on a liturgical meaning, but, two days later, I only saw shiny black men twisted by the flames, posing so obscenely in death that they looked as though they might even upset the good ladies of Palma and their distinguished confessors."

Death had become the master in Majorca.

Death. Death. Death. As far as the eye could see.

In spite of his anguish and revulsion, Bernanos tried to remain lucid. Come what may. "You are a brother in tragic lucidity," the dramatist and poet Antonin Artaud wrote to him in 1927, almost the only contemporary of his to have liked his book *L'Imposture*.

Lucid in his opposition to cowardice and silence.

Lucid because he forced himself to look horror in the eye and chronicle the very crimes the Francoists sought to conceal.

In contrast to the Republicans, who posed for posterity in front of the churches they destroyed and the dead nuns they had just murdered (photographs that shocked the world), the Francoists were careful not to broadcast any images of the violations carried out by *el terror azul* ("the blue terror", the colour of the Falangist uniform).

These were, of course, precisely the violations Bernanos chose to describe.

It was a question of honour, he said, that old sense of honour which is now deemed rather reactionary, something rooted in childhood. (Today's inner-city youths would no doubt understand what he meant.)

He decided to write about the violations he could see around him because he was not a delicate soul (though he regretted it) who wrote for readers with delicate souls (and he is a great writer as a result).

He decided to write that the oft-repeated slogan of the Catholic Church, *LET US LIBERATE CHRIST'S TOMB*, no longer meant anything but the systematic murder of suspects.

He decided to write that the Nationalists had instituted a regime of terror, blessed and encouraged by the Church even as it piously uttered: *Accipe militem tuum, Christe, et benedice eum.*

"A regime of terror," Bernanos wrote, "is a regime where the powers-that-be judge it lawful, normal even, not only to aggravate the character of certain crimes by tricking transgressors into breaking martial law (holding up a clenched fist is punishable by death, for example), but to take pre-emptive action to exterminate dangerous individuals, or rather those suspected of becoming so."

Bernanos warned: "a whole people are in need of salvation. We cannot stand by while the Nationalists wipe them out."

He addressed the bishops directly, his trademark irony tinged with desperation: "But, no, my Excellencies, I am in no way accusing your venerated brother, the Most Reverend Archbishop of Palma. He was represented at the ceremony, as usual, by a number of his priests" – who, supervised by the military, offered their services to those facing imminent execution, promising them absolution.

The war had revealed the Spanish Church's true and terrifying face.

For Bernanos, the point of no return was at hand.

2

José bumped into Manuel on his first day back in the village. Manuel had shared his friend's enthusiasm for the revolution in July, but then found it too hard to part from his family. José told him in the minutest detail about his time in the big city and the extraordinary thirst for change he'd witnessed there. He said nothing of the quarrels between the various factions. He said nothing of the lying propaganda spewed by the political commissars with their Russian accents and round-rimmed glasses. He said nothing of the sniggering of the two murderers in the café on las Ramblas, as if suppressing these things could help him stifle them in his own mind, as if skipping over them could prevent him from falling apart.

Manuel had been more than receptive to José's ideas in July, but now he listened dejectedly, his friend's words reminding him of a distant and near-forgotten period of his life. He had gone back to his old habits, anxious to shake off his former excitement, terrified at the prospect of having to match up to the grandiose ideals that had enthralled him.

Everything he had loved and defended a month earlier now left him cold.

Worse than that, he disavowed it all, dismissed it outright.

To justify himself, Manuel listed the string of accusations he'd stored up against his former comrades over the last two weeks, most of them irrational and unfounded: *They were drunks, borrachos, layabouts, poofs who stirred up their own shit with the sole aim of satisfying their libidi, libidi – what's the word? – libidinous instincts, that's it, and they were far too earnest, which meant they were playing straight into the hands of the Nationalists.* With this bunch of prejudices and lies, Manuel had conveniently trampled the truth. (José soon realised his accusations had spread like a virulent strain of flu throughout the village.)

José felt utterly disarmed by this unexpected rejection.

So disarmed that he didn't have the strength to defend the cause he'd embraced in Lérida.

Yet again he had underestimated the changeability of men, their capacity to turn.

He had misjudged the human need to defile and vilify the beautiful things in life.

Once more, he regretted his artlessness.

But still he hoped. There is nothing as stubborn and dogged as hope, especially groundless hope. It is like a weed clinging to a rock.

He thought it was too early to backtrack. Too soon to surrender. Yes, hope is a tenacious weed.

His optimism had taken a knock since the so-called

"Unforgettable Days" and his idea of revolution was now stained with an ever-growing shadow of doubt (*Or rather it had eroded,* I say to my mother, *the more he yearned for it, the more it shrank, what we call "a peau de chagrin" in French. Oh yes*, she says, *I love that expression*), but still something in him, from his past dreams, refused to die.

José decided to pull himself together.

Pretending he didn't care if it worked or not (he didn't want to come across as incorrigibly naive), he told Manuel of his plan to help educate the illiterate farmers of the village. They were being deliberately kept in a state of backwardness that some (namely Diego) were shamelessly exploiting.

Manuel shrugged. He hardly bothered hiding his scepticism. He tried to convince José to join the group led by Diego rather than splinter off into some half-baked scheme of his own. He was going to come a cropper unless he was careful. *Cuidado con el pelirrojo. Watch out for the redhead.*

No. José was adamant. He'd rather die than join Diego. Of that he was sure. All power, he was now certain, was oppressive by its very nature. He wouldn't repeat the same mistakes as his Anarchist comrades in the city. They had weakened themselves by taking part in the regional government and were now caving in on all fronts, compromising on everything.

What struck José most forcefully from his conversation with Manuel was how important Diego had become in his absence.

Almost all the local farmers, he learned, had rallied to his cause. Those who had been the most vociferously opposed to

Communism were now praising him. The bootlickers were flattering him: *You are the man of the moment.* The shit-stirrers were out to please him too, belittling anything the Anarchists did. The most obsequious farmers were falling over themselves to shake Diego's hand with Marxist–Leninist zeal. And the mothers of the village were worshipping his balls with a new kind of devotion, because that's what mothers do, they worship the big chief's *cojones* (according to my mother).

José guessed that his own father had become one of Diego's disciples.

It was a stab to the heart.

While José grew gradually more morose in the village, Montse and Francisca, many kilometres away, were being swept up by the pleasures of city life. The revolutionaries had decreed that a free glass of water should be served to anyone in need of refreshment, and every evening the two young women sat on the café terraces and watched the sun go down over the city roofs.

One evening in August, a Wednesday, Montse was alone at Café Aurora, the place she'd been the very first evening she arrived in the city. At a nearby table, she saw the young Frenchman who had recited the poem about the sea.

Our eyes met, greeted one another, se saludèrent, my mother says, *amour rose up in the air, it was love, pure love, there and then.* And she starts singing a little ditty:

> *Las naran las naranjas y las uvas*
> *En un pa un un palo se maduran*
> *Los oji los ojitos que se quieren*
> *Desde le desde lejos se saludan.*

The young man asked permission to come and sit at her table. My mother agreed without too much fuss (any revolutionary worth her salt had to spurn chichi niceties, phoniness and simpering, in short any manifestations of bourgeois affectation).

The young man was called André. He was French, but spoke impeccable Spanish. He was just starting out as a writer and had left Paris the week before. He was waiting to be drafted into an International Brigade to fight on the Aragonese front. He'd arrived, from Perthus, in a filthy, packed train, but he had quickly forgotten the foulness of it thanks to the happy commotion in all the compartments. As a flask of white wine was handed from person to person, the train filled with rallying cries and hoarse singing, insults aimed at Franco, *that son of a great whore and his gang of bastards, el hijo de la gran puta y su pandilla de cabrones.* Something dark and exalted spread throughout the train, as if collective fear had been flipped on its head, transformed into triumph, but with its darkness still lingering. André had been met on the station platform by a bevy of *guapas*, their delicate, feminine arms laden with flowers, and led to the Continental Hotel, where he was staying for next to nothing (the service was excellent though).

He told Montse he was ashamed of France, ashamed of

126

Europe. They had let Hitler stomp all over them. Shame on the Catholic Church, too, for prostituting itself for the army.

He was leaving the following morning.

He was free that evening, and the whole night.

Montse fell for him immediately, from the very first moment, completely, utterly, and permanently (for those who might not have guessed, this is what's called love).

They decided to go and see a film. All cinemas had stopped charging an entrance fee since the Anarchists had taken over the city. The second they sat down they threw themselves on each other. In the dusky cinema, they exchanged a first impassioned kiss that lasted at least an hour and a half. It was Montse's first ever kiss, and with it she made her grandiose entrance into the world of sensual delights, in front of a screen filled with other kisses, doubtless a lot more proficient, but likely more subdued too.

All the old rules had gone by the board since July. It was as if morality now followed desire, as if traditional constraints no longer applied. Everyone (or nearly everyone) in the city had cast off their shackles without a grain of conscience (but with a touch of worry nevertheless), which is why Montse, after an hour-and-a-half kiss, the sweetest thing ever to happen to her, and without a moment's hesitation, agreed to accompany the Frenchman to his hotel room. She didn't have the time or the mind to wonder whether her underwear was suitable for the occasion (she was wearing a particularly unappealing pair of large cotton knickers with a matching camisole). The couple promptly tumbled onto the bed in a sensual embrace, breathing in each other's skin, stroking each other, legs and arms entwined. To cut a long story short, they made love with an intensity and urgency that made them both shudder . . .

They broke apart, gasping, sweating, and looked at one another, as if for the first time. They remained quiet for a moment. Montse asked the Frenchman when he had to leave. He ran a finger round the contours of her face, as if lost in contemplation, and said something she didn't understand. He had a *shivery voice, all quivery, I won't forget it* (my mother's words). She asked him to repeat what he'd said. He did, and again she didn't understand, or rather she did, but without grasping the words (for those who might not have guessed, this is what's called poetry).

At seven in the morning, the Frenchman looked at his watch and hurled himself out of bed. Time had shot by. He was already late. He got dressed in a rush, kissed her one last time, and ran to join the soldiers waiting to take him to the front.

Montse skipped back to Francisca's in a state of elation, of almost unbearable joy, a joy that lifted her up off the ground, *como si tuviera pájaros en el pecho, as if there were birds in my chest*, a joy she would have liked to have shouted about from the rooftops. It was, quite literally, spilling out of her eyes. When she walked into the kitchen, where Francisca was busy cleaning, her sister looked at her with a puzzled expression, as if Montse's essence were altered all of a sudden.

What's happened to you?

I'm in love.

Since when?

Since last night, and now for life, for ever.

That's quite a grand statement!

It's the season for grand statements, Montse replied, beaming.

As she was dying to tell the entire world about her new-found happiness, she told her sister about her encounter with the Frenchman and the hour-and-a-half kiss which had reached down into her soul (or reached up, depending on where the soul is supposed to reside), skipping over the caresses and fondling in the hotel room and everything that followed on from there.

In the days, the months, and the years afterwards, Montse never stopped thinking about the Frenchman (he never sent any news for the simple reason that she had not had time to give him her surname or address). How had he slept? What was he eating? Was he thinking of her as she was thinking of him? On which front was he now fighting? Was he cold? Hungry? Was he frightened? Was he dead or alive? She would never know, and she asked herself these same questions, again and again, thousands of times, for the next seventy-five years.

Her period didn't come on time. Days went by, and still it didn't come. Montse had to admit she was well and truly *embarazada*. The Spanish word for "pregnant" seems far more eloquent in this particular instance. Montse was *embarazada* with André Malraux's child (that is what my sister and I ended up calling him, after the famous French writer and statesman who fought in the Spanish Civil War. His real name remains a mystery to this day). Montse had heard her brother rejoice at the news that abortion had been legalised. He said it was going to contribute vastly to the emancipation of women. She thought about it for a little while, but a part of her resisted such a choice. She put off the decision, day after day.

Francisca began to suspect there was a problem. Montse normally sang from dawn to dusk, but now she barely said a word (my mother had a prodigious talent for singing and I'm sure, with the right guidance from an impresario, she could have made a name for herself, carved out a career in the world of music, especially since her talent would have been boosted by her great beauty. Speaking without any self-interest, of course, such a career might have also allowed her to make some money and opened a few doors for me). Montse now sat with her head in her hands, so absorbed in her sad reverie that the dishes she was cooking kept burning, her chickpeas reduced to cinders. In fact, Montse only realised when a thick smoke filled the kitchen. *Are you upset about Mamá?* Francisca asked, worried by the frequently burned food.

Montse recognised she had indeed forgotten her mother despite her promises to keep in touch.

Yes, she said, bursting into tears.

Francisca hugged her, which made her twice as upset. After a good ten minutes of crying, with tearful words spluttered incomprehensibly into her sister's neck, Montse confessed she was pregnant and that she only had one option left: suicide.

*

Once suicide had been discounted (quite quickly), Montse decided not to stay a moment longer in the city. An irresistible, almost animalistic, urge was driving her back to her mother, even though she knew full well what was going to happen: there would be moaning, weepy prayers accompanied by a continuous stream of *Dios mío*, pleas to the Blessed Virgin Mary and the Infant Jesus, interminable sighs of *and-what-are-people-going-to-say?*

On a grey afternoon in October – exactly two months since she'd cheerfully left for the city, and six days after General Millán Astray had shouted "DEATH TO THE INTELLECTUALS, LONG LIVE DEATH" at Miguel de Unamuno, the rector of Salamanca University (a call to murder that became the Nationalist's rallying cry) – Montse returned home to her village with a child in her womb, a radio in her bag, and the certainty that the beauty of summer was gone for good.

The instant she saw the first houses at the edge of the village, a childish need to cry choked her throat. She told herself that a part of her life was ending and she was giving up happiness and youth for ever.

It was as if she'd left the village in a bygone era, in another life, when she'd been part of a wholly different story.

She found the village austere, dour in the extreme, and its emptiness made her own presence all the more visible, outrageous even. The gossips and busybodies observed her from behind their half-closed shutters.

She walked down the steep street where her family lived, pushed open the stable door and climbed the stairs. The living room seemed desperately ugly to her with its shabby wooden chest and the crucifix hanging on the wall above it (a cross her mother had refused to remove, for once forcing her husband and son to back down. They had ended up giving in to her stubbornness, reckoning it better not to contradict the whims of a housewife with an underdeveloped political conscience). Montse wandered like a stranger into the house where she'd been born.

Her mother burst out of the kitchen and threw her arms around her daughter. *¡Hija de mi alma, déjame que te mire! Let me look at you!* She studied Montse a long while: she'd seen her leave as an awkward adolescent and now she was returning a young woman in the full flush of youth (*a little too full*, her mother joked, pointing at her belly). *My goodness, you've changed! My goodness, you're beautiful.*

José, who had just come in from the fields, didn't seem too pleased to see his sister. He asked her rather rudely why she'd returned home so soon. *We only have one mother*, Montse stammered. *One too many*, José said. *Shut up!* their mother snapped, pretending to take her shoe off and hurl it at him. Her brother and mother had obviously gone back to their bickering old ways. For reasons she couldn't fathom, this comforted Montse a little.

The following morning, after a sleepless night spent wondering how, and when, she was going to tell her mother about the pregnancy, Montse decided not to delay her confession any further. Nerves jangling, having just emerged from her room, she told her mother she was expecting a child and that the father had died on the battlefield – this version of events felt nobler and slightly more palatable than the simpler truth.

Everything she'd dreaded then occurred. Her mother collapsed into a heart-rending lament: Montse was casting shame on the whole family, sullying their reputation, in fact there was no greater dishonour than this, and, from now on, people would point at them in the street, drag their good name through the dirt. And if word of this got out her father would kill her.

That's exactly what I'm hoping, Montse said coldly.

This curtailed her mother's screaming, but not the forlorn sighs, the appalled grimaces, the repeated exhortations not to say a word to anybody, and the anguished prayers to Jesus, and the Virgin Mary, for a solution. (The answer didn't come from heaven in the end, but from a much more earthly encounter: we shall deal with that when the time comes.)

Bernanos, in the meantime, was still busy mulling over the events that would haunt him for the rest of his life, indelibly shaping his faith.

The Church's shockingly criminal behaviour, its cynicism, duplicitousness and sickly caution, had – paradoxically – inspired him to yet greater and more passionate affirmation of his faith in Christ.

His Christ, however, was not magical, as Montse's mother believed. Nor was he vindictive and on the constant lookout for misdeeds, as doña Pura was persuaded. He was even less the bully that the Archbishop of Palma had banked on.

Bernanos' Christ derived directly from the Scriptures. He saved beggars, forgave thieves, blessed prostitutes, the poor and the excluded, indeed all impoverished souls dear to his heart. He was the Christ who admonished the wealthy young man: *Sell your riches and give them to the poor.* For goodness' sake, all one had to do was read the Scriptures. He was the Christ who despaired of those who spouted words and did little else, those laying burdens on others' shoulders while sitting around idly themselves. *All you had to do was open the Scriptures at any page and it was all there, written in black and white!* Jesus scorned those tempted by illusions of grandeur, the attention-seeking dignitaries who gorged themselves on food at the rich man's table while delighting in being addressed as "master".

Bernanos' Christ is remarkably similar to the brotherly figure imagined by Pier Paolo Pasolini. He, too, portrayed Jesus and his followers as the poor and the homeless, men and women without hearth or tomb, today's refugees.

Christ was not crucified by Communists or the sacrilegious, Bernanos observed with his biting wit, "but by opulent priests encouraged unfailingly by the bourgeoisie and intellectuals of their time: the Scribes".

So, did these basic tenets have to be taught all over again to the Spanish clergy and their flocks?

What had the devout flocks been doing with God's grace? Was it not meant to open up the heart to love? Wasn't this grace expected to shine forth like an electric light bulb? Where the hell did these secretive believers hide their love of the poor?

Did it need to be explained to them again, with church bells ringing, that Christ himself had lived among the poor? St Francis, *il Poverello* himself, chose to announce the kingdom of the poor on the roads of Umbria. "The devout are a cunning lot, though. They did not dare say a word while Saint Francis wandered through the land with his companion, Saint Poverty, at his side. But once he was dead, what do you know? They were all so busy honouring him that poverty somehow got left out of the celebrations . . . those priestly scoundrels in their purple and gold robes had got away with it again!"

For Bernanos this was the worst kind of deceit.

And because he dared to write about it, he would be accused of aiding and abetting the Communists in their fight against the Nationalists (the latter, of course, were supported by his former friends).

It took Montse only two days to realise that the atmosphere in the village was even more oppressive than she'd feared. The joyous upheavals of July had spawned a feeling of mistrust. It contaminated all relationships down to the most intimate. She couldn't say what it was exactly, but there was something noxious and putrid in the air. It stuck to the walls, to the earth in the fields, to the trees and sky, every element of the landscape.

She had found the happiness of freedom so intense, but now she was experiencing the hell of being trapped. The control habitually exercised by everyone on everyone else in the village had intensified dramatically and she thought she might wither under the constant scrutiny. Even if she spent her entire life in the village, she knew she would never get used to the gossip again. All it took was for a young girl to light a cigarette for the event to be commented on for weeks; the same was true of certain "women's diseases", though the gossip became even more convoluted in these cases as, like the body parts affected, nothing could be openly mentioned by name. That would have been not only inappropriate but also frankly obscene.

Rosita told Montse most of the villagers had rallied to Diego and his clashes with her brother had become so violent that some were predicting a terrible outcome.

The fact was those two had nothing in common, nothing to agree upon.

They were opposites, my mother says, *eran la noche y el día. Like day and night.*

One was as old as the other was young, though not in the literal sense, of course. José was hotheaded, impulsive, quick to explode, twitchy, brittle and chivalrous. Diego was calm, driven by a need to control events and himself. He assessed and weighed up every action; gauged, measured and calculated every decision (my mother: *Maybe I'm being unfair, this could sound unfair*). José's sensitivity made him vulnerable, more vulnerable than anyone, it tormented him. Diego's sensitivity hardened him, nurtured his indifference, sealed him from the world. José's knowledge did not come from any schooling, it wasn't the product of some family fortune. It had just been brilliantly garnered from reading the odd book and newspaper, here and there, whatever he could lay his hands on. Diego always exercised his intelligence to combat something or someone, rejecting his father's knowledge, as, he said, it only served to reinforce the arrogance of his caste (*maybe I'm being unfair*). So, while José rebelled against chicanery and the kind of underhand dealings favoured by some politicians, Diego inched forward, one step at a time, scarred by the violence of his early years, mistrustful of people, of everyone, without exception, fully aware of the compromises needed for his painstaking intrigues.

So, what you're saying is that one embodied the poetry of the soul, while the other embodied realistic prose, I say to my mother, giving in to my own inordinate weakness for flowery statements.

Something like that, algo así, my mother says.

José had got carried away by the utopias he'd encountered in Lérida, in those days of burning skies. Diego, probably because he was lacking in confidence, put more effort into moulding himself to the existing order (*the hideous order of the informers and overseers*, José said, mirroring Bernanos, even though he'd never read him). Diego liked tough, stubborn projects, nice square ideas. And, in José's presence, by some kind of reverse pride, he had a tendency to exaggerate this humdrum streak and bring up the most boringly pragmatic matters. Armed with the hammer of dogma, Diego banged on about the utmost importance of political realism (the very realism that José, like Bernanos, believed was the common sense of bastards).

But secretly (in my mother's humble opinion) Diego was

jealous of José's insolence, his startling beauty, the flights of fancy that turned his eyes to fire, and his thirst for chaos, which both seduced and repelled him. Diego (again in my mother's humble opinion) was deeply envious of José. It was a dark jealousy, mysterious and wild, an infatuation even, and he didn't know how to rid himself of it.

Events would confirm my mother's theory.

At the end of October, having pondered over and over the shameful, appalling news of her daughter's pregnancy, Montse's mother came to find her in the attic bedroom where she spent whole days at a time. Her mother told her with some glee that she had a plan, but, for the time being, she could say no more. Staring blankly into space, Montse didn't ask any questions, or demand to know more. She showed no curiosity at all. All Montse could think about was her Frenchman. She could think of nothing else and didn't give a damn about the rest. She didn't give a damn if people were murdering each other, if the French prime minister Léon Blum had refused to help Spain and if Britain, worried about clinging on to her status as a world power, had done the same. Montse didn't give a damn about the things that made her brother despair, namely that the Spanish government had been prevented from buying weapons from private firms and had, therefore, been forced to seek help from the Soviet Union, the only state willing to accept Spanish gold in exchange for arms. *All these things* (my mother says) *were the least of my worries and I didn't give them a moment's thought, I didn't give a stuff about them, je m'en tamponnais l'oeil, I'm sorry to admit.*

A week after her mother's mysterious announcement, and as she carried on cracking hazelnut shells with heavy stones – a form of relief from her melancholy, if nothing else – Montse heard a knock at the front door and then the sound of her mother racing down the stairs, and racing up them again, with Diego in tow.

Montse was so surprised she couldn't say a word at first.

But Diego, who had never dared speak to her before, not even dared brush past her or hold her hand during a Sunday *jota*, announced he was delighted to see her again, cracking hazelnuts rather than living in the city where things were quickly going awry. Montse gathered her thoughts.

She found Diego had changed.

His face didn't seem as closed as before. It was softer, less obstinate, and his shyness wasn't as paralysing, even though his cheeks reddened a little at the sight of her.

They exchanged platitudes while Montse's mother left them alone for a moment to fetch some plum brandy from the kitchen.

Taking advantage of her absence, Montse began to think very fast and very intensely, and before she even knew what was going to come out of her mouth, she asked Diego if he knew.

He immediately understood what she was alluding to. *Yes*, he said, blushing. They fell silent. Montse was relieved and, quickly changing the subject, asked what news there was of the war – Diego was always the first to hear anything in the village.

Franco, apparently, in a great show of mercy, had asked

Yagüe, the butcher of Badajoz (he'd already executed four thousand Reds in the city), to ban the practice of castrating soldiers. Evisceration and decapitation were now the only authorised methods of punishment. *We're still holding on to Madrid though*, Diego said. He was proud of the fact that such things hadn't come to his knowledge thanks to some fanciful village rumour, but because he received official communiqués and had equally official use of channels of communication like the telephone – he was always ahead of the local rumours by about two or three days. Diego spoke of *us* and *our* soldiers, *our* war, *our* difficulties, *our* chances of victory, as if these things belonged to him. Montse found it a little irritating.

She was unable to sleep for nights following this brief encounter contrived by her mother.

Should she agree to her mother's secret plan? Agree to marriage? Because this was about marriage, even though neither she nor Diego had uttered the word.

Should she agree to marry a man she did not desire, a man who had never touched her, apart from with his eyes? A man with a harsh face and hair the colour of a cow's tail, a man whose speeches to the village were filled with practical, angular words that made her anxious, though she would have been hard-pressed to say why? The words "efficiency" and "organisation" shot out of his mouth like bullets from a gun. *I'm exaggerating*, my mother says, *but you understand what I mean?*

How was she to agree to such a marriage when she would

have given her life to get her Frenchman back? Montse still harboured the unreasonable hope that André would return from the frontline and whisk her off to France where they would live happily ever after with their child.

She thought of the Frenchman day and night, incessantly, and mourned how circumstances had robbed her of the chance to know him. She didn't have a photograph of him. She knew nothing of his childhood, his tastes, his foibles or failings, the relationships that had fashioned his personality. She didn't know his surname, and, because of that, even employing the single-mindedness of a detective, her searches would have come to nothing. She knew their encounter had been preordained though, and she loved him with a love as great as the pain destroying her. She kept seeing his face leaning over her, and her reflection caught in his eyes, and the strand of hair across his brow that he swept away with a movement of his head. Then the star-shaped scar dug into his left cheek where she'd left the softest kiss. His absence ate away at her heart.

She was so preoccupied with this love she didn't notice the coldness of the attic or the first kicks of the child inside her womb. She sometimes even had the hallucinatory sense that her lover was there, right next to her, for a few seconds, before fading into the shadows. Days went by and Montse went on hoping André Malraux would appear out of nowhere and save her. *Please God may he return*, she whispered to herself, though she inwardly questioned the chances of such a mad wish.

She spent three months living with this desperate hope, and

for three months her mother stealthily, drop by drop, injected her with the poison of her unhappy blackmail. Montse thought she'd die if the Frenchman didn't find her.

Her belly was swelling, the pile of empty hazelnut shells was growing, but still the Frenchman didn't appear, and still she carried on living despite herself.

Eventually she had to admit the Frenchman was never going to find her. All hope was dead. He would have to live on in her mind. *I dreamed of him for years, ma chérie, years and years.*

She had four options to consider:

She could commit suicide by jumping from the attic doorway into the farmyard.

She could live as a single mother, *une fille-mère*, as they said in those days, as an outcast, a *desgraciada*, with a child who would be called a bastard (Rosita's cunning idea of making the village believe the child had been conceived without any male intervention, by a process known as parthenogenesis in scientific terms, or by the grace of the Holy Spirit in Catholic terms, seemed highly problematic).

She could flee back to the city, give birth anywhere, find a job and leave her baby with a childminder of some kind.

She could accept the marriage proposal: a calamity that was less cruel and perhaps more tolerable than the previous three calamities.

Finally, because she still wanted to live despite it all, and because of her mother's constant pressure, she accepted this last option.

After countless tussles with her conscience and her heart, swallowing back her tears, she agreed to the marriage, an arranged marriage if ever there was one.

She was not only agreeing to a marriage, she was agreeing to a name, to a safe position, to a certificate of respectability. In exchange, she was being asked to sacrifice her short-lived youth and her hopes of ever finding love again.

Her mother cried with joy. *Praise be the Lord* (He had been remarkably assisted by her clandestine machinations, but such things were best not mentioned). Her daughter was to be wed to a *señorito*, a young man of means! Her daughter, *praise be to God* again, was going to become part of a family whose way of life was envied by all. *What luck, the bliss of it . . .*

With an ugly man, Montse said, dampening her mother's enthusiasm.

Men don't need to be beautiful, her mother said.

So, what are they meant to be?

Men, that's all. Ser hombre y nada más.

And there the argument ended.

Montse's mother was giddy with pride at the idea of her daughter becoming a member of the well-to-do classes. She would now, thank heavens, spend the rest of her life with refined people. She proudly announced the news to her neighbours:

What good fortune! they said in unison.

What a lucky girl she is.

She'll not want for anything.

She's set up for life.

She's struck gold.

This enthusiasm, of course, was tempered the moment Montse's mother turned the corner, each neighbour chipping in with a comment:

The poor girl is going to get it with that family!

She's got her work cut out with doña Pura, what a dragon!

What about doña Sol? She's as sad as a pile of stones.

And that big house is like a cold tomb, no thank you.

I say it's better to be poor and happy than rich and unhappy.

This last pronouncement was immediately endorsed by all the neighbours present.

I'm not sure exactly how, but these remarks, as reported by my mother, seem to overlap with a passage of Bernanos' writing. I quote him from memory: "The wealthy despise those that serve them, either through conviction or foolishness, as ultimately they only believe themselves to be defended by the corrupt; they only put their trust in the corrupt." Thinking about it, these remarks strike a direct chord in me, too. I'm becoming aware, a little more each day, that my avid interest in my mother's accounts, and Bernanos' writing, stems from their relevance to my present life.

The hardest part was yet to come for Montse. She had to tell José about her forthcoming marriage.

José had only had one idea on his mind since returning from the city: to do as much as he could to thwart Diego's increasingly

Stalinist ambitions, to stand in his way whenever possible. But he had to admit that he had very few resources for the task, and Diego was at a distinct advantage. Juan was the only ally he could count on. José still had one card left to play, though. He could become the troublemaker: he could walk upside down on his hands and refuse to go along with Diego's games. Whacking Diego in the face was another option he didn't want to discount.

José had a profound contempt for authority, sectarianism, playing safe, the kind of rigidity Diego exemplified. It was a biological, incurable contempt and it made him resort to all sorts of brazen behaviour in Diego's presence. He liked to imitate the cackling of chickens during meetings, raise two fingers like the Devil's horns and sing *rumba la rumba la rumba la* or put his hand up as if he were at school, saying, *Before undertaking any kind of intellectual endeavour, just remember to repeat exactly what you've been told!* This led to much childish chuckling, which the villagers strongly disapproved of.

Diego couldn't stand these repeated affronts to his authority and virility. They wounded him more than any genuine challenge based on facts. No-one was particularly surprised, therefore, when the tragic events of December came to pass.

But for you to get it, so you comprendes bien the chain of events (my mother says), *you have to understand the violence that existed between Diego and José. It went right back to their childhood days. I'm going to have to give you an entire anthill crawling with details, une fourmilière de détails.*

*

In 1924, seven-year-old Diego came to live with his family for the first time. Don Jaime insisted he went to school in the village. Believing it to be wholly appropriate, and because she was fascinated by all things British, doña Sol decked the boy out in a tidy, mid-season navy-blue blazer with gold buttons, a crown suspended over two embroidered reclining lions on the breast pocket. This conspicuously elegant jacket had an immediate effect: the other boys of the class, themselves of rather doubtful cleanliness and dressed in threadbare, cobbled-together clothes, hated Diego the instant they saw him. José was already the playground ringleader and he brutally excluded the newcomer from all skittle games at break time under the pretext that the little *señorito* might spoil his fancy costume. Diego's self-esteem took a knock and he remembered it for the rest of his life – it was a wound that stoked up all the other wounds he'd received during his early years. From then on, Diego hid behind a wall of pride, refusing to join in any games with the children who had shamed him, preferring to remain alone during break times rather than risk being mauled by the group. He'd learned from a tender age, though tender is not really the word for his childhood, not to give pain or humiliation an opportunity to take hold.

José carried on with this cruelty, not only excluding Diego from skittle games, but calling him a little girl, *chiquita* and *señorita*, or shrimp, teasing him about his carrot-coloured hair, flaunting his scorn in a thousand different ways. Though he had no serious motive for his dislike, José stuck to his aversion. It was not so much an aversion to what Diego was, but rather to what he symbolised. Perhaps, without José being fully aware of it at the time, the dislike was about Diego belonging to a ruling class which was refusing to relinquish its colossal privileges, something he loathed instinctively.

The tension between the two boys ended in fights over the most minor things and often for no reason at all. Each time, José was astonished to discover the viciousness of Diego's punches. Nothing, from his anaemic complexion to his scrawny buttocks or coat-hanger-thin shoulders, suggested such ferocious determination. As they rolled around on the ground hitting one another, José understood that Diego's cold fanatical fury, along with his unpredictable brutality and overbearing urge to win, meant he would one day, come what may, get what he wanted.

Diego was used to dealing with his unhappiness alone. He didn't mention his ordeals to his family, but he pointedly refused to dress in smart clothes again, even for his first communion. He became more and more withdrawn at home, steadily more aggressive towards his parents, particularly the woman he secretly called his wicked stepmother.

Diego settled into loneliness in the cold and gloomy Burgos house with only the lead soldiers and toy tanks his father had given him for company. In this dark solitude he resolved to distance himself from those closest to him. This distance was to remain in place all his life.

As a teenager, Diego began again to seek out the company of other boys his age, and, intriguingly, this included José. At the time, all the boys of the village wanted to be like José. All wanted to walk on their hands like him (exactly what he proposed to the farmers in his village in 1936). All the boys wanted to mimic his way of dressing (badly) and his hairstyle (which was also pretty bad). They wanted to imitate his natural fearlessness, his instinctive courage in the face of adult authority, not to mention his impertinence towards the priest don Miguel, who was bent on depriving him of Holy Communion. Everyone wanted to ape José's snide remarks about the backward village, with its backward peasants, and his own half-wit, backward father who shat himself bending over for the degenerate Burgos son who presumed to lord it over them all.

Still Diego sought out José's company, tried to get close to him for any spurious reason, wanted to urge his friendship on him. In all sorts of ways, he attempted to seduce him.

But, each time, he came up against José's steely, implacable stubbornness, a pride fuelled by the hardships of his background. And more often than not José, unfairly and crudely, simply cut Diego dead, a look of disdainful pity on his face.

Diego was obviously hurt by this. It may have been that joining the Communist Party was his way of making José realise he had got him wrong. Yet by the time war broke out, Diego's party membership only exacerbated their differences. Their banal and childish enmity, relentless as it was, but without serious effect, was suddenly transformed into a political hatred, the most violent of all hatreds, the most insane.

By November 1936, the two young men could only function by thinking and acting in direct opposition to one another.

José said he far preferred chaos and the natural fragility of things to the monstrous order established by the Bolsheviks (an order that Diego readily accepted without protest or hesitation). José continued to champion the idea of collectivising farmland and declared his confidence in the Durruti column. For him, Stalin's promises to send weapons to the Anarchists if they agreed to organ- ise themselves militarily were nothing but despicable blackmail.

Diego trusted Order and Institution. He supported the regular army and wholeheartedly believed in the Soviet Union. Since setting himself up in the town hall, he had begun, amongst many other lofty endeavours, to write a weekly bulletin for those at the highest levels of authority. He had grown fond of drafting reports, and his love of paperwork was such that he often wrote several bulletins a day. He noted that the village remained calm thanks to its inhabitants' common sense (despite threats from a small group of well-known troublemakers), and his writings were annotated with a host of mundane and superfluous details about the village: timetables, schedules, journeys, clothes, pranks, reported conversations, drinks consumed, etc. He tweaked all propaganda pamphlets with the same meticulousness, not hesitating to lambast the schemers secretly working for the enemy. He organised literacy campaigns that amounted to gathering the peasant masses in the main room of the town hall to: (a) vaunt the integrity and discipline of the Communist militiamen; and (b) warn the above-mentioned masses of the danger posed by local troublemakers – no prizes for guessing who was being singled out there.

Needless to say, the farmers present at the meeting – as always a prudent and cowardly bunch of arse-lickers – felt obliged to applaud. *Temor – Fear, – and submissiveness, which are generally masked in peacetime, become more visible in wartime*, my mother says, philosophically. *You should have seen how people cheered Maréchal Putain in the first years of my guided tour of France*, she adds with a note of humour, (not only for her muddling of the French for whore *(putain)* and Pétain – which in this instance was probably intentional – but also because, from 1939 to 1940, my mother and my sister Lunita were catapulted from concentration camp to internment centre, improving no end their geographical knowledge of France. All of this is still remarkably clear in my mother's mind).

In an effort to assert his power, Diego pronounced the words *Patria* and *Pueblo*, "Motherland" and "People", with great solemnity. He scolded Carmen, the town hall secretary, for the most trivial matters, proudly cut the ceremonial ribbon for the inauguration of the school canteen, and with policeman-like zeal he checked the width of the potato peel Rosita left behind when preparing the school children's meals. He was overbearingly bossy with the four young men who assisted him, although they seemed more than ready to accept the authority of someone other than their father. He made them carry out the most pointless tasks – such as counting the number of customers in Bendición's café. He decreed the end of religious feast days (his aunt developed dizzy spells from the distress), replacing the Day of Epiphany with a Day for Children. He summoned so-and-so and so-and-so from the village to ask them how they spent their days, what errands occupied them: checking they were all they claimed to be. And he made sure to leave his shiny Ruby revolver in full view on his desk so that dialogue in the office remained as one-sided as possible.

From the moment he took up his official role in the town hall, Diego seemed to be driven by something implacable, something cold and hostile, and it led people to fear him.

Unlike everyone else, José refused to be intimidated by this martial behaviour. Diego's shiny gun did not impress him, nor did his over-polished shoes or the words that fired from his mouth like bullets. He made it clear to all that when he went to the town hall to telephone Francisca he was going to get news of his sister rather than receive orders.

My brother, ma chérie, was not a ... what's the word?

Coward? I suggest. *A yellow-belly?*

Oh, you do make me laugh with your ridiculous words, is that even a word? my mother says.

Diego received José with calculated *froideur*, or rather with the frosty delight he imagined true leaders customarily displayed, speaking in brisk, gruff sentences, the way true leaders spoke (or so he believed), in essence he exhibited all the hallmarks of what he considered to be true leadership: impatience, uncommunicativeness and chronic sullenness.

Comfortably settled into the former mayor's office, where

he'd hung a large portrait of Stalin, and despite the intimidating airs he put on, Diego seemed to experience an intense thrill when answering the telephone (*his orgasme bureaucratique, my brother called it,* my mother chuckles) – as use of it was an irrefutable sign of power and the town hall the only place in the village to have a telephone.

By this stage Diego and José's animosity had already reached its lowest point (and marriage to Montse was not yet even on the public agenda). *This is going to end badly,* many people warned.

One morning in November, while both of them were eating tomatoes and grilled peppers for lunch in the kitchen, Montse decided to tell her brother.

José?

Yes.

I need to tell you something.

What?

You're going to be cross.

I love being cross.

I'm going to marry Diego.

That's a good one! José laughed, not believing a word of it, and he came out with a proverb, *Te conozco bacalao aunque vengas disfrazao,* which means something like *Don't think I can't see straight through your lies.*

Seeing his sister's serious face, José changed his tone.

Don't tell me you're serious.

Montse nodded awkwardly.

But that's horrendous, he shouted. *You're going to bury your-self alive with that carrot-topped bastard. With that cabrón!*

José had gone white.

That Stalinist shit-head.

The very one. Montse gave a little a smile in an attempt to soften the atmosphere. The corner of her mouth froze, and her brother flew into a rage.

That piece of shit?! he screeched. *That traitor, that son of a whore, that dandy?!*

He was beside himself, face now bright red, hands trembling, the veins in his neck all swollen up.

That bastard is only after your arse, he yelled, *he's scum. He has an accounting book instead of a heart* (it took Montse years to forget that particularly harsh comment).

I beg you not to ruin everything, their mother said.

Who's ruining everything? José bellowed. *Me, or you with your shady dealings?*

Diego is a serious boy, she pleaded feebly, in the hope of defus-ing her son's anger. *He has a good heart.*

This set him off again.

That hijo de puta, is everything I hate the most in this world. He kills everything that's beautiful. That's why he killed the revolution and he'll kill my sister, he'll kill her, he will.

Their mother blanched. She resorted to stating what she be-lieved was an inescapable fact: *Your sister has to get married, that's the way it is, full stop.*

My sincere condolences then, José said with a terrifying laugh.

At this, Montse burst into tears and tried to run out of the room.

José grabbed her sleeve.

Why are you crying? Because you're selling yourself like a whore to the highest bidder? You're right to cry: it's a disgrace.

Don't talk to your sister like that, their mother commanded.

You, you old pimp, you don't have a leg to stand on, he shouted back.

Mother fled to the kitchen while Montse raced up to the attic and threw herself on the bed, sobbing.

José remained alone, his anger pouring out into the room. He shouted at himself like a madman, saying he reviled marriage. It was just a form of legalised whoredom, and any old fucker could afford to take a girl as his wife, any old piece of shit had a legal right to get himself a maid, a free maid at that, and for life. At least when you were a worker, under the orders of a boss, you got paid, for fuck's sake. This marriage lark was insane. He ranted a bit more to himself, pacing up and down the room his mother laughably called the sitting room, kicked a chair which had been irritatingly left in the wrong place, yelled obscenities till the house shook, jumped down the stairs, four steps at a time, charged up the calle del Sepulcro, muttering even more, and burst into Juan's house. His friend was reading a newspaper, and before he could lift his eyes from his page José had started shouting at him, then at his brother Enrique – *What are you looking at?* He cursed his pimp of a mother (who wasn't there to answer back), then Franco, then Mola, then Sanjurjo, then Millán Astray, then Queipo de Llano, then Manuel Fal Conde, and Joan March, then Hitler, Mussolini, and Léon Blum, Chamberlain, the whole of Europe, and then the greatest, biggest bastard of them all: Diego Burgos Obregón.

Give me a beer, Juan, por favor, before I bloody kill that son of a bitch.

In Palma, all forms of insurgency had been stamped out.

The people of Majorca were numb, despite thousands of murders of unspeakable savagery and the sickening harassment of the wives of those who had been executed (notably a ban on widows wearing mourning).

Bernanos said he would need to fill pages and pages to explain why these facts, which were never doubted by anyone, ended up generating no reaction at all. "Reason and honour made one wish they were not true, but the senses had been stunned and shut down. A kind of resignation that dumbfounded executioners and victims alike."

Bernanos had discovered that when fear takes hold, words become frightened too and emotions are held in check. A howling calm then settles in, providing ringleaders and criminals with the perfect cover.

Montse's and Diego's parents met on November 10. A wedding date had to be set and decisions made on the dowry (my mother: *It was pretty measly.*) The contract between the betrothed needed to be worked out (Montse's father signed it with a cross). The meeting was a torture for Montse, and not, as some might think, because her destiny was about to be permanently sealed, but because she had to witness her clumsy, timid parents in the lavish Burgos drawing room.

Montse's father had placed his cap on his knees. A distinct line divided the pale upper part of his forehead from his tanned brow. He looked apologetic in his chair, lumpy, fat polished shoes neatly tucked one against the other. He had the hesitant, helpless gaze of a beaten dog, despite doña Sol repeating: *Please make yourselves at home* and *No need for any fuss between us*. Montse's mother – raw-boned, eyes lowered, reddened hands clasping each other in the folds of her black skirt – was trying to disappear and had almost succeeded.

Montse studied her parents in silence, with a deep but painful intensity, as if observing them for the first time. She found herself thinking, *How humble they seem.* Their faces, their hands, especially their hands – her mother's chafed and damaged from washing clothes with bleach, her father's bulky and calloused, nails black with earth. It was not just their hands, it was their gauche gestures, their little muffled laughs, the exaggerated deference and unending gratitude. All of it revealed the poverty of their lives, a poverty handed down to them over the centuries.

Montse understood how similar she was to them. However hard she might try in the future to wear make-up or expensive clothes, or bedeck herself in precious jewels, or mimic the gestures of superiority, waving maids away like bothersome flies, she would always retain the same air of humility. It was embedded in her, immutable, indelible, a kind of permission for others to commit abuses and humiliations of all sorts, a look she'd inherited from generations of impoverished ancestors. It was etched on her face, carved into her flesh, the passed-down residue of constant submission, demeaning surrender, stifled revolt, a firm conviction that men and women like her counted for nothing on this earth. Montse realised she wouldn't have the courage to watch her parents wriggling uncomfortably again, embarrassed and ashamed of themselves, in the company of her self-assured parents-in-law. Whenever possible, she would do her best to avoid gatherings at Easter or Christmas, anything that might bring the two incompatible families together.

On the eve of her wedding, on November 21, 1936, to be precise, just as Montse was putting the finishing touches to her dress (white with red flowers, I still have it), José burst into the kitchen in a state of despair.

Durruti's been assassinated! They've killed Durruti!

Durruti was José's ideal, his partner, his poetry, his reason to worship: Durruti the rebel, the pure, Durruti the guide, the generous. He attacked banks, kidnapped judges, captured a truck packed with the Bank of Spain's gold and gave it to the strikers in Zaragoza. Durruti, often imprisoned, sentenced to death three times, expelled from eight countries, and now a myth thanks to his assassination.

As José walked around in a daze repeating, *They killed him* (as if his brain were refusing the information his heart had instantly absorbed), Montse couldn't help but think she had put so much energy into hoping something bad might happen, wishing for a diversion, a disaster, something as seismic as the July revolution to free her from her marriage and change her destiny, that, though aware of the absurdity of it, she found herself wondering if she were in some way responsible for Durruti's death.

José held back his tears as best he could, but he was soon overwhelmed and started to cry like a child.

Montse could not remember ever seeing her brother cry and she was soon consumed by hopelessness too. It got even worse when José – in an attempt to shake off his pain, to cheat it and detach himself from it – shouted tearfully at his sister:

And don't count on me tomorrow! There's no way I'm going to be part of your wedding masquerade. I won't dirty myself by mingling with an accomplice to Durruti's murder!

On the day he learned of Durruti's death, which he blamed squarely on the Communists, José hastened to the town hall to confront Diego.

According to village gossips, Diego had grown more tolerant of others after his first meeting with Montse, and certainly since the news of his engagement to her had been made public (the announcement had spread like wildfire through the village). This change in mood, the busybodies said, was proof of love's notoriously mollifying effect. It was said Diego had become more accepting, and had even pushed his new-found tolerance so far as to address his startled stepmother, doña Sol, as *Mamita* in front of witnesses (she couldn't believe her ears). As for his future brother-in-law, Diego had promised Montse (during a second meeting engineered by her mother) that he would reassess his opinion of José, forget his past provocations and wipe the slate clean. He was now prepared to accept José, not in any warm way, of course, but in a less hostile manner.

So, when José charged into the town hall on November 21, 1936, to accuse Diego (in front of his four young employees) of being a vile accomplice to Durruti's murder, Diego allowed himself only a slightly concerned expression and carefully avoided replying, much to everyone's surprise.

The wedding was celebrated the next day. Without José. Almost without a bride – certainly a bride with a headdress, a veil, a bouquet, a procession, bridal bells or bridesmaids. It was only a wedding ceremony by name, one not ushered in by a traditional period of engagement, nor due to be followed by a traditional honeymoon either. The ceremony bound together two young people who had never really spoken to one another, still less courted one another, two people who had made a pledge to keep the same secret their whole lives (Diego making Montse swear she'd never say he wasn't the child's father, and Montse promising, on her mother's life, that she'd keep quiet about the whole thing, though she pointed out the lie would be obvious to anyone who could count the months of the year on their fingers). One of Diego's assistants rushed through the formalities in five minutes flat, declaring the couple man and wife, joined in matrimony, until death did them part (this footnote was thrown in at the last minute to compensate for the overly brief nature of the ceremony).

Diego refused to wear a suit, despite doña Sol and doña Pura's combined pleas. Instead, he wore a dark canvas tunic that made his red hair look ablaze. Montse noticed that the insides of his ears were thick with tiny tufts of ginger hair.

Montse's father dressed in the dark suit he'd worn for the first time at his sister-in-law's funeral eight years previously. It had a lingering smell of mothballs about it. Montse's uncle, whom everyone called Tío Pep, wore a similar suit. Her mother put on her special black taffeta dress with a white collar. She had dreamed of a big wedding with all the conventional formality and found it hard to hide her disappointment. Doña Pura covered her head in a lace mantilla scarf (*an excellent idea, for everyone's sake*, my mother tells me). As for doña Sol and don Jaime they were exquisitely dressed, as always.

Montse had gone along with it all as if a part of her were absent from the proceedings, otherwise engaged, aware of the details but no longer involved in them. Montse recalled the moment they exchanged rings because doña Pura suffered from a fainting fit and had to be seated on a bench, her mantilla lifted, her blanched cheeks patted back to life to rid them of the disapproval she could no longer repress. Montse recalled the moment she said *Yes* too, because she was thinking how she'd have to get a divorce if the Frenchman did come and fetch her one day. She was ashamed of her thoughts.

The wedding lunch was served in the Burgos dining room.

Don Jaime had not revealed his attitude to the union. He had not voiced any objection or shown any reluctance (as opposed to doña Sol who'd had a minor breakdown upon hearing the news). Don Jaime was no longer astonished by the oddities of human behaviour, particularly his own son's. He seemed to accept this misalliance as just another feature of it. As a sign of goodwill, however, he uncorked the champagne and proposed a toast to the newlyweds.

The guests (ten in all, including the witnesses) clapped and turned to Montse's father, waiting for his toast. He remained obstinately silent, staring at the floor, his hefty, knotted hands placed on the table, a sudden shyness preventing him from delivering the naughty joke he'd prepared that morning – perhaps stifled in his enthusiasm, too, by the proximity of doña Pura, supremely dignified in a long black silken dress. During the course of the meal, Montse's father did not exchange a word or nicety with his austere and glacial neighbour. It was no doubt his embarrassment at his incapacity to speak which led him to drink more than he should have, despite his wife's admonitions not to overdo the wine or wipe his mouth with his sleeve. When pudding came he stood up in front of his petrified daughter and struck up a bawdy song, *Look how my thingy wiggles up and down, up and down, fíjate cómo se mueve mi cosita*, but he immediately got the words all muddled up and fell back into his chair, doña Pura giving him the sort of frosty smile that would have cut off even the most articulate orator.

As he attempted to pull himself together, Montse's mother jumped to his defence, saying, *It's the emotion of it all!* Thinking she'd found a plausible justification for her husband's behaviour, and fretting he'd be seen as an uncouth boor in the company of *such posh people*, she repeated, *It's the emotion of it all!*

Montse had quivered at her father's ogre-like behaviour for more than fifteen years, had always seen him as a tyrant, irascible and harsh. He was the man she feared the most, who'd threatened to throw José out of the house for daring to voice a different opinion, the father who'd shouted hundreds of times, within the four walls of the family home, that he'd never lick señor don Jaime's arse, and how one day he'd tell the rich bastard what was what. Yet on her wedding day, Montse discovered a perfectly harmless, impotent father, meek and stuttering, eyes fixed on his plate, fearful of everything.

The guests all shared a concern that political issues might be brought up: the smallest remark about such-and-such an organisation, and its role in the war, risked upsetting the lunch at any moment. Everyone was acutely aware of the fact.

Indeed, all the Spanish political parties of the time were represented by the guests at the table, each confident in the legitimacy of their cause, each animated by the most noble sentiments, convinced, within the limits of their experience and their vested interests, that theirs was the only valid viewpoint. All of them, if necessary, were ready to shake up and shatter anyone else's mistaken beliefs. The master of the house, don Jaime, was suspected of having Nationalist sympathies. His sister doña Pura, when alone, swore by Franco and the Falange. The bride's father was part of a Socialist union of small landowners. The groom was not long converted to the Communist cause and Montse had become infatuated with her brother's Anarchist ideals, just as you fall in love with a song or a person, a sort of infinite yearning for poetry.

All the major political currents of Spain in 1936 were present at the table, and their incompatibility, on a national scale, would, by degrees, eventually lead the country to ruin.

Montse's first months of marriage in the large, sad and cold Burgos house were amongst the most testing of her life.

I was like a patched-up, rickety chair in a Louis Quinze sitting room, my mother says. *If I could have buried myself away in a mouse hole I'd have done so. You know, basically, c'est simple, I was only alright when I was shut away on my own in the lavatory.*

Montse felt out of place, as if she clashed with her new surroundings, and she was miserable because of it. She'd been thrust, unprepared, from the harshness and poverty of peasant life into the unfamiliar world of the land-owning classes. She told herself she had to suppress all spontaneous gestures in order to avoid appearing vulgar, had to force herself to eat as little as possible to appear more refined. *Would you like some cake? Just a crumb, por favor.* She spoke in long-winded, overdone sentences, driven by the naive assumption it was good manners not to call a spade a spade. She feared seeming coarse, heavy and ungraceful when she ate, moved, laughed and talked, as such things unfailingly betrayed the humbleness of a person's origins more than any curriculum vitae. Montse was no longer Montse.

Constantly alert to any reaction from the Burgos, who treated her with unexpected courtesy, she dreaded *causing any sort of bother* to the members of the family. Their roles seemed to be shared out with mathematical precision and she always thought she was committing some gaffe by getting their respective duties or positions muddled up.

She tried to stick to her place in the pecking order, or what she perceived to be her place, carrying out the unassuming tasks she imagined were expected of her, busying herself with the cleaning (the revolution had swept away her official role as maid, granting her the vicarious, but more advantageous, position of wife). She humbly swept the floor, humbly cleared the table, humbly put the china away, anxious to put every utensil in its designated place, any change in the relative positioning of objects potentially upsetting the balance of the whole household. And the house's domestic order, of course, was nothing but the faithful translation of doña Pura's own soul, its crowning glory.

The courage Montse had drawn upon in previous months, when she'd hatched escape plans or thought about throwing herself off rooftops, vanished abruptly into thin air. She was drained of all strength. She'd become *a rag, nothing more than a mop, a fregona*.

In December 1936, Bernanos was told of an incident which he relates in *Les Grands Cimetières sous la lune*. Afraid of reprisals, a

Republican mayor of a small town in Majorca had set up a hiding place inside an empty water tank close to his home. He took refuge there every time he heard the faintest sound of footsteps. A purge squad, however, learned of his presence thanks to a highly patriotic tip-off. They dragged the mayor out of the tank, shivering and feverish, and led him to the cemetery where they shot him in the stomach. As he tiresomely took a rather long time to die, his inebriated executioners went and fetched some plum brandy. They poured it down his gullet, and then smashed the empty bottle over his head.

"My heart is broken," Bernanos said. "That is all there is left in me to break."

How can I hang on? How can I survive? Montse wondered in the large and musty Burgos house. Things were not going well for her.

She still found it hard to dismiss her first encounter with don Jaime from her mind (the time he'd made his little remark). He hadn't exactly charmed her.

Now he adopted a tone of courteous respect, a degree of aloofness on the rare occasions they spoke, the sort of distance he maintained in all relationships – the distance he kept from himself. (She understood later how don Jaime's natural tactfulness prevented him from showing her any overt sympathy, and that he refrained from revealing his innermost feelings to anyone in his family.)

Montse felt like an idiot in his presence.

The man intimidated her, just as he intimidated all the people in the village.

They thought he was eccentric, unpredictable, extravagant, but they were fond of these traits. They forgave them, deeming them to be typically aristocratic whims: his posh clothes for a start (he had not succumbed to the fashionable worker look of the time), his leather gloves, his felt hat with the initials J.B.O. on the rim, his incomprehensible love of books (they said he had more than seven thousand, but how did he remember everything contained in them?), and then his limitless knowledge (they said he spoke three languages, that he knew the names of a dozen planets, and even the Latin term for chickpeas – *Cicer arietinum*, for those who don't know).

He was a *bon vivant*, jaunty, delightful, not half as rich as he liked to think he was. Affable and respectful too, with everyone, including his wife, though he remained neglectful of those religious matters so beloved by his fanatical sister. He was generally stable in his moods, and fundamentally cheerful except when it came to his son who was *as prickly as a stretch of barbed wire* (my mother's words). He was friendly with the villagers, joking with them at any opportunity, enquiring about their olives and hazelnuts. He had a word of comfort for everyone and knew the names and ages of all his employees' children. *Don Jaime*, the farmers said, *is a gentleman, but he doesn't take himself seriously. He's natural, uncomplicated.*

From the very outset of the war, in matters concerning his sister, don Jaime maintained an attitude of patient forgiveness, such as one might adopt with a turbulent teenager. Sometimes, though, he ended up mocking her: *If the Reds could hear you, they'd give you a good hiding, or perhaps even rape you.* Doña Pura just turned her back on him without saying a word and stomped off, shaking with indignation. Or she shrugged with disdain, heartened by an article she'd read that morning in her newspaper: the *Nuremberg*, a battleship flying a swastika, had just sailed into the port of Palma. Finally, a piece of good news.

In all affairs relating to the management of his lands, don Jaime blindly trusted his foreman Ricardo. This young lackey – as José called him – had a bony face and quivering eyes. He'd been taken on as a teenager and showed a genuine reverence and attachment to his employer (excess servility, Diego called it). He looked after the fields with love and pride, as if they were his own, bending over backwards to satisfy all demands made of him, secretly flattered by his master's respect. The young man was just as devoted to doña Pura. Every Sunday Mass, he carried a small white bench for her to place her feet upon – a humiliating function (in the etymological sense, too, as he had to reach down to the humus, to the ground, for her comfort). Of course, he became an object of ridicule for José and Juan, who unsurprisingly gave him the nickname of El Perrito, the lapdog.

Don Jaime was a real thinker, my mother tells me.

He spent hours locked away in his library. Montse had never seen anyone read for their own pleasure before. She was yet more paralysed with awe in his presence.

He spoke a *castellano castizo*, an old-fashioned Spanish, although he spiced it up from time to time with the odd melodic swear word. It seemed to Montse that the brilliant, easy and spiritual words of his conversations shone as luxuriously as the *objets d'art* in the house. They impressed her in just the same way. They were indisputable proof of his distinction. So, in order to try and keep up with him, at least to become his studious pupil, to improve herself in a rather pretentious way (*basically fart higher than my arse, histoire de péter plus haut que mon cul*, my mother says, not wanting to miss a chance to use one of her all-time favourite French expressions), Montse poshed up her words when speaking to him, made them sound all stiff and starchy – in the same way her old teacher, sister María Carmen, liked to use delicate Catholic euphemisms: *Please go and wash your hands* instead of *Go to the toilet*, or *So-and-so went to heaven* instead of *So-and-so died*, or even *Respect the Lord's teachings* instead of *Shut up*.

Montse was even more uncomfortable in doña Pura's presence because the good lady winced every time her manners were seen to be wanting – all the time, in other words. One day she wrapped a pair of dirty shoes in a copy of *Acción Española* (my mother: *a rag to wipe the shit from your culo with*), and doña Pura, who worshipped the newspaper as if it were something sacred, said to her brother: *Poor little thing, she has no values. No surprise really, given where she comes from.*

Even though doña Pura repeatedly told her, with a sort of Christian sweetness thick with threat, *This house is your house, young lady*, Montse became so clumsy around her she often wanted to flee, but where to? It was freezing in the house, and everywhere else was just as cold.

My feet were caught in a trampa, my mother tells me.

In a trap?

That's right, I was snared.

But credit where credit is due. Doña Pura was welcoming this penniless peasant girl into her home, a girl who ate bread rubbed with garlic, who licked her knife at the end of every meal, who didn't even know how to play bridge. All she'd learned in life was how to crack hazelnuts and squirt milk out of ewes' udders. And the girl's own brother worshipped a modern Antichrist whose hordes of primitive devotees paraded around in their undershirts. *Poor, poor Spain.*

Despite her migraines, doña Pura found time to talk to Montse. Nothing more than idle chit-chat, of course: the girl had no conversation. But doña Pura was a charitable soul and was prepared to be generous. For the love of Christ she could accept many sacrifices. She was comforted, however, by the thought that this civil marriage tying her nephew to the peasant girl wasn't really worth the paper it was printed on. She would only have to put up with the young woman until their inevitable divorce.

Yet slowly, perhaps because of her innate romanticism, doña Pura began to take an avid interest in Diego's unnatural liaison with the pauper girl. Their relationship almost seemed as if it had been lifted straight out of one of her romantic adventure stories, like *La Guapa y el Aventurero*, a novel where love transcended social barriers. It was a rousing, entertaining book, instructional too. It made her cry as it somehow managed to find the labyrinthine routes to her heart. She read it at night, between articles from *Acción Española* and verses of the New Testament.

It became doña Pura's holy mission, although she didn't want to attempt anything too ambitious, to give this coarse and rather crude girl some basic manners, the rudiments of an education: so she could, at least, elevate herself, perhaps not to the level of her husband, but certainly a couple of notches below.

This holy mission, though occupying an important part of her time, did nothing to appease the pains racking her disappointed flesh. When Montse asked how she was feeling (the way you do with people to whom you owe respect, but without feeling any genuine sympathy), the apparently moribund doña Pura said with frightful meekness ladened with hidden meaning, *I'd prefer not to talk about it right now*, and carried on applying a handkerchief dipped in vinegar to her brow to relieve the migraine burrowing away at the lobes of her brain.

This was one of doña Pura's ways of revealing the agony of her illness but also the extreme care she was taking not to inconvenience those around her. Lest anyone should forget she was suffering in silence, however, she let out regular sighs, dug up, it seemed, from the very depths of her being, all this while swallowing a spoonful of syrupy tonic with a grimace of disgust.

Montse presumed it necessary to display the required level of compassion, but in her mind she wanted to shriek, *Shut up, just shut up or I'll break your bones.*

Speaking of which, my mother says, *can you get rid of the cough medicine in the fridge? It's bringing back bad memories of doña Pura.*

Montse often sought comfort from doña Sol at the beginning of her time in the Burgos household. She thought she'd found an unexpected ally in her, and doña Sol was quick to cherish Montse like a long-lost child.

Doña Sol had once hoped for children of her own, a baby from her own womb. She had prayed to the Virgin Mary, burned dozens of candles, sipped eight different kinds of herbal tea, eaten nothing but rabbit for a while, worn a string of scapulae, and consulted the best doctors in town as well as the village midwife. All to no avail. *You cannot imagine,* my mother says, *what the shame of being infertile was like back then, how it was for infécondes women in those days.*

Doña Sol had counted on Diego's arrival curing her of this atrocious defect that had deprived the marital bed of its sweetest fruit, but in many ways it only made matters worse.

When Montse arrived in the Burgos house, young, beautiful and as fresh as the morning, the child-starved doña Sol behaved as if the girl had been sent from heaven. She transferred all her excess and frustrated tenderness onto her.

Actually, it was not so much a transfer as a flood.

Not a day went by without doña Sol foisting her affection on her in some way. She cooked her *mantecados* (shortbread), her favourite kind of biscuit, prepared her cups of afternoon hot chocolate so thick a spoon could have stood up in them. She implored Montse for her company with hungry eyes, rushed to find her as soon as she heard any noise in the kitchen, detained her in the drawing room with pointless questions. She attributed all sorts of wishes to Montse and then set out to fulfil them, spoiling her outrageously in those days of extreme hardship, giving her the latest high-heeled shoes, shiny necklaces and all sorts of accessories Montse chucked to the back of the cupboard in her bedroom. Doña Sol then monitored tiny changes in Montse's moods, waited for a compliment, gently reproached her for the reserve she interpreted as a form of rejection . . . in essence, doña Sol succumbed to the flow of maternal love she had painfully suppressed for more than twenty years, letting it spill over uncontrollably.

Montse, who had initially been grateful for the attention, was soon suffocating. The flattery, the fits of generosity, all the presents given with such urgency – essentially desperate appeals for love, a form of silent begging – brought Montse no pleasure at all. In fact, they made her anxious. Even if she forced herself to be as genuine as possible when receiving these unwanted gifts and said, *Thank you, that's very kind of you*, she found it difficult to express any real joy.

I couldn't manage to fake it, really, do you see? my mother says. *I couldn't reassure her that her cakes were the best in the world, or come up with all those marvellous déclarations children make to their mamans when they're sad and in need of love.*

Montse tried to eke out a bit of pity, a bit of kindness for this fragile, broken woman, ravaged by frustration. *My heart, though, in those days,* my mother says, *and forgive me for being so very crude, but it was dry, as bone-dry as the inside of doña Pura's cobwebbed chocho.*

Sometimes, out of boredom or exhaustion, Montse went along with the farce.

At other times, she could take no more of it and shunned doña Sol altogether.

One day, as doña Sol was launching into a discourse on the immeasurable delights of motherhood, Montse replied coldly: *Mother hyenas also give birth to baby hyenas and they don't make a big fuss of it.* Doña Sol burst into tears. My mother remembers this clearly because she suddenly wanted to be absolutely ruthless towards this woman who was exploiting her sadness so as to squeeze a few drops of affection from her, *No! no! y no!*

Even though she refused to let herself get sucked into doña Sol's life, and even though she was incapable of feigning tenderness, Montse also knew she could not afford to offend doña Sol. She had to use judicious doses of friendliness in harness with her calculated coolness. Often all these inner struggles came to nothing, however, and Montse had no choice but to lie. Putting on a contrite face, she came up with excuses such as an urgent trip to Rosita or a visit to her ailing mother. Then she ran into the countryside, as if she were being chased – and it was true in a way, she was being chased by her guilt, her regrets, a feeling that she had built a cage for herself, but most of all by a voice in her head saying, *This is no life, this is no life, no es una vida.*

She invented headaches to curtail the coffee-time chats meant to fill the women's afternoons, and retired to her bedroom which had become a sort of airlock chamber. She lay on the mahogany king-size bed and got lost in her thoughts – if one could define the sort of fleeting, hazy ideas she had as thoughts. They blew through her mind like draughts of air, transient concepts, ephemeral fragments, each one gone without trace. Bored beyond anything she had previously experienced, Montse looked at the purple light falling on the olive groves or followed the trajectory of a trapped fly (*just like me*, my mother says) as it banged against the windowpanes (*just like me*).

She invented sad things for herself. She imagined her mother falling down the stairs and dying or her brother getting knocked down by a car (there was not much chance of that as there were only two cars in the village: don Jaime's Hispano-Suiza and the clapped-out truck driven by Juan's father). She imagined herself sobbing behind a hearse, a solemn crowd walking beside her, all dressed in black. Or she spoke to herself as lonely children do until a noise from the drawing room made her aware of what she was doing.

She filled her days with the following (in order of importance):

(1) knitting light blue slippers (garter stitch) for her baby boy;

(2) indulging in fantastical dreams about her musical

career. These involved plans to escape from the village and meet up with her favourite singer, Juanito Valderrama, though the pair of them invariably ran into problems such as Juanito having to join the Republican army;

(3) reading Bakunin's book. Her brother had lent it to her in July and she'd hidden it under a pile of sheets in her bedroom cupboard. The book had the knack of sending her to sleep in two seconds flat;

(4) visits to her mother, who gave her revolting advice on how to tie and untie a newborn baby's nappy, *like this and this*, followed by tips on how to examine the child's stools, with particular attention to their colour and consistency, and how to wash, wipe, dry and apply talcum powder to the baby's buttocks, and other distasteful matters;

(5) secret chats with Rosita about the "Act", which she now considered to be another inconvenience, but was that normal? Were there any pills she could take? Should she pretend to moan with pleasure? *Think of Jean Gabin*, Rosita said (he'd been their heart-throb since they'd seen him in the film "La Bandera"), *or just finish him off with your hand*;

(6) visits to Maruca, the grocer's wife, to engage in depressing conversations about the president of the Republic, Manuel Azaña, a lazy lump and a wimp. *What the hell was he waiting for? Why wasn't he making the rich fork out and pay their dues?*

(7) speculation about what could be upsetting her brother

other than their argument about Diego. (Why was he always up in arms about everything? Where did his despair come from? Was it something he carried inside him or was it a reaction to external events?);

(8) many anxious thoughts about why her husband was so obsessive, though she knew she lacked the basic facts to explain this obsessiveness and could it be explained anyway?

One day, my mother and I sit and watch tennis on the television: Nadal versus Federer. Nadal tugs compulsively at his shorts every so often and this prompts my laughing mother to list Diego's various oddities, his pet subjects, his tics, his bizarre whims and above all his fixation on cleanliness, a DESPOTIC fixation if ever there was one, as it led him to disinfect his hands twenty-five times a day, to glide an obsessive finger across his desk to track down the merest speck of dust, to change his shirt every morning (at the time, in Spain, this was a sure sign of mental disorder) and to wash his feet every blessed evening (the norms of the time meant a weekly, if not a monthly, washing of feet was more than sufficient. Besides, an aversion to soap and water was seen as an undeniable sign of virility: *real men had stinky feet*).

As obsessive about order as cleanliness, Diego took the utmost care to tidy his trousers away before getting into bed, folding them in half on the back of a chair, legs meticulously checked and straightened so they were of equal length (this exasperated Montse so much that in an act of silent defiance she just chucked her clothes around her, willy-nilly). Diego folded and tidied his things in the way he marshalled his emotions, demonstrating an extraordinary capacity for self-control, notably holding himself back from asking Montse the question that had been burning away at his lips for months, a question that haunted him incessantly (he admitted this to her much later on): did his wife still love the man who had made her pregnant?

Diego's various manias, his craving for order, for hygiene, his psychological as well as his physical constipation, his long periods sitting on the lavatory, only added to the reluctance, reserve and reticence Montse felt towards him (*all these words of yours beginning in "r" really do seem a little over the top, ma chérie*, my mother says), and this despite the fact that she told herself endlessly, to convince herself, that her honour had been saved (her own mother's exact words) and that she should be eternally grateful.

Despite her best efforts to suppress and conceal it, Montse's reticence vis-à-vis Diego manifested itself regularly. It was all the more noticeable as he was surprisingly tender and loving with her (though still as cold and haughty with everyone else). In truth, Diego was very happy with Montse, he delighted in her. He was filled with pride at the idea that she had entrusted him with her life.

Often he prevented her from slipping past him and gently held her by the wrists, proffering a red-bearded cheek for *a besito, one little peck, you have to pay to get past*, but Montse nearly always managed to wriggle out of his embrace, claiming there was some domestic matter requiring urgent attention.

Montse would then feel guilty that she didn't love her husband as he would have liked, the man who had saved her from dishonour, perhaps even saved her full-stop, guilty, too, for not feeling up to the responsibilities of marriage that her mother and aunt Pari so highly valued. And although she was only just sixteen, she felt guilty, also, that she was too exhausted and too old, or so she imagined, to love another man again.

She just repeated to herself: *This is no life, this is no life, this is no life, no es una vida, no es una vida.*

It was not much of a life for Bernanos in Majorca either. That seems obvious from reading his book.

In March 1937, he decided to leave Palma, boarding a French ship with his family. Too many crimes had been committed on Spanish soil, too many crimes infected the air.

He thought he had just seen the lowest circle of hell.

He had observed the Most Reverend Archbishop of Palma wave his beneficent hands over a shipment of Italian machine guns. "Did I see that or not?" he wrote. He had heard men shout "LONG LIVE DEATH" hundreds of times. He had seen "the well-trodden paths of Majorca receive their deathly harvest of deviant thinkers: workers, farmers, members of the bourgeoisie, chemists and notaries".

He had heard one man, someone he believed was on the side of the murderers, tearfully confess to him: *It's too much, I can't take it anymore, they've just done this,* and then describe another hideous crime. Bernanos saw how many of the newspapers, in their vileness and cowardice, stayed perfectly silent about the Francoist atrocities. "There is something thousands of times worse than the viciousness of brutes," he wrote, "and that's the viciousness of cowards."

He had read Paul Claudel's poem, its stanzas setting his saintly admiration for the purges to verse: "eyes filled with enthusiasm and tears", and so on. Shakespeare, surely, would have simply called Claudel a son of a bitch (or some Shakespearean equivalent).

Bernanos had seen honest men turn to hatred, people who had finally found an opportunity to think themselves superior to others, or at least their equals in wretchedness. He wrote a sentence which could have been written this very morning, so relevant it seems to our present-day world: "I believe my greatest service to honest men is to warn them against the imbeciles and bastards who cynically exploit their deepest fears."

He tried for as long as he could to hold on, not out of bravado, not even in the hope of being helpful, but out of a sense of solidarity with the people of Palma, because he shared their anguish and absolute terror.

By March he could take it no longer.

Bernanos left for France with a dark foreboding: the horror he had seen, but had been unable to arrest, was perhaps only the foretaste of other horrors to come. He wrote this: "I will not tire from repeating this: one day, we, also, might undertake the purging of the French nation, copying the Spanish example, with the blessing of our clergy too. Do not worry, Their Excellencies whisper in my ear, once things are under way we will turn a blind eye. But, Excellencies, that's exactly what I want to avoid."

Bernanos dared to identify the future evil, even if he risked being booed by the optimists still hoping for some sort of way out, but all they were doing was stirring up hot air, looking at the world through rose-tinted spectacles to avoid taking pity on those less fortunate than themselves. While he, Bernanos, was stating the basic facts.

He dared to identify the future evil and paid dearly for it, but, as we all know, he was proved right. Three years later Europe would tip into a horror that exceeded anything yet seen.

As that horror brewed, and because he dared to speak freely in a world that wasn't free, Franco put a price on the writer's head (Bernanos narrowly avoided assassination attempts on two occasions). In France, his last dispatch on the Spanish Civil War, published by the magazine *Sept*, was censured by the Dominicans, and he was accused of propagating Communist ideology.

The writer André Gide, it should be noted – who had taken up the Republican cause – was being accused of treachery at the same time for having criticised the Soviet regime in his book, *Retour de l'U.R.S.S.* (published in 1936). All forms of fanaticism are alike.

In Spain, the same accusation of treachery was directed at those who dared to question Communist methods, however timidly. Luis Cernuda, León Felipe, Octavio Paz, to name but a few, were put under surveillance, interrogated and brought to heel by the Russian representatives with their round-rimmed glasses, keen as ever to rectify the least supposed deviancy.

Bad times for Bernanos.

Bad times for those who questioned allegiances of all kinds and preferred to trust their conscience rather than the prevailing dogma.

Montse's life had begun to brighten. She saw glimpses of light on the horizon, some benefits to her new world. A couple of swallows had built a nest in an outbuilding and she interpreted this as a positive omen. Never had spring seemed so sunny.

Diego, who was ordinarily of Spartan abstemiousness in all things, and who didn't drink or smoke or eat to excess, came teetering home one evening, stinking of whisky. He found Montse in the bedroom and threw his hairy ginger arms round her neck. Staring into her eyes, he asked her if she was happy to be his wife.

For a second she wanted to say, *I don't know*, but seeing him so serious, almost begging, she changed her mind and said, *It's alright, it's alright.*

Wanting to hear it again, Diego pushed her further: *Really?*
It's alright, it's alright.

He did not feel the need to hear any more than that.
If you're alright, then I'm alright.

Montse was deeply grateful he hadn't tried to explore her uncertain feelings any further.

Little by little, she became less harsh with herself, more generous with her husband, vowing to love him better. She didn't instinctively tend towards unhappiness and getting stuck in a rut of gloomy thoughts was unnatural to her. So she leaned into life again. She rediscovered the notion of time, something she had lost since the *month of splendour* (what she called the enchanted month of August 1936). She regained the look of goodness that don Jaime, only seeing the fear within it, had mistaken for humbleness a year before (a common mistake, by the way, as many like to knock basic goodness, seeing it as a virtue of the simple-minded and the dim-witted). Montse rediscovered her *enlightened goodness*. This was not an innocent's goodness, nor that of a simpleton, nor even that of an angel or a self-righteous prude, it was a forward-thinking benevolence, freed of illusions about the depths to which men will stoop in order to get what they want, and it was determined to triumph over those depths.

Montse's life was restored to an even keel in the spring of 1937, although the war rumbled on and arguments regularly flared up between Diego and his father.

I should emphasise at this point that, despite Diego's admiration for his father (mixed with resentment), which he was at pains to conceal, and in spite of don Jaime's longstanding silent affection for his son, a form of barrier still separated the two men.

For years, father and son had shut themselves away in a pathetic incapacity to communicate and neither seemed willing to mend it, scarcely exchanging three words a day, their mutual incomprehension as firmly entrenched as the habit of saying good morning and goodnight.

With the beginning of the war, this innocuous friction between father and son gradually became layered with violence. Although the nonchalant don Jaime was of a peaceful disposition, the tension between the men reached new heights. Their clashes were frequent. Their once silent and unexpressed hostility exploded at the slightest provocation. The smallest thing led to violent altercations. Could one trust the foreman or not? Was it polite to use a toothpick at the end of a meal or not? Should October 12, the Day of the Spanish Race, the *Día de la Raza*, be celebrated or not? The least thing was a trigger for bickering, irritation and conflict, and this although both knew that the real causes of their differences lay elsewhere.

When dinner conversations drifted towards the war and how it might be won (*war*, my mother says, *was the spoken and unspoken topic of every single conversation*), Diego, who could not conceive of any opinion other than his own, accused his father of turning his back on his century, of dipping his toes into the dangerously murky waters of feudal Spain. *The world has changed*, he shouted at his father. *It's no longer the country of your childhood. Your farmers don't want to be treated like slaves anymore, and one day they'll chase you from your lands.*

Don Jaime shook his head, while his wife and sister looked on aghast, and Diego revelled in his provocations.

Every time he listened to his son, don Jaime realised he was getting old. He was no longer sure of the validity of the ideas he had espoused in his youth – when politics still interested him. As a young bourgeois with leftish leanings, don Jaime had believed in a kind of friendly humanism. It had the clear advantage of not eroding a single one of his privileges, and meant that he could deplore the oppression of the people, and the inconsiderate abuse of power by the moneyed few, without giving up a single *peseta* of his own, while bestowing, too, on the intellectuals and poets the task of expressing his profound outrage at the widespread deprivation in his country.

Don Jaime's clear-sightedness and intellect meant he refused to choose between three irreconcilable standpoints: his casual, student-day progressiveness; his family traditions (embodied by his sister doña Pura); and the inflexible doctrines of a leader like Stalin (which only bred heinousness). For don Jaime, these views (Anarchism didn't tempt him in the least either) were equally filled with deceit and bound to fail. In fact, he thought that to be part of a dogma, a cause or a system was the surest way for a man to become a criminal. He was suspicious of everything. Yet Diego often told him that not to take sides at all, when war demanded that everyone make a stand, was a typically reactionary way of ducking responsibility. It was a rich man's cowardice, a luxury, a surrender flatteringly dressed up as scepticism.

In defiance of his son's aggressive censure (it upset him more than he let it be known), the insinuations of many (all the man cared about was his money) and political pressures from all directions (he had to decide what faction he supported at some point), don Jaime was the only person in the village who refused to take sides. Certainly the only one in the village to recognise the madness of men and their era.

This withdrawal, as much down to don Jaime's character as his social position, outraged Diego and led him to even harsher criticism. His father's finely calibrated detachment from the world eventually fell apart.

My mother remembers father and son nearly coming to blows over some fried eggs. Don Jaime claimed you had to pour a larger quantity of oil in the pan for the egg whites to get brown and crispy, while an indignant Diego maintained foodstuffs had to be used sparingly in times of war. *You don't give a damn about this or anything else so long as you get the income from your land*, he said to his father. Don Jaime sprang to his feet, his son a second later. The two of them stood face to face, measuring each other up, like sparring cockerels.

Don Jaime, who was usually so calm, and who ordinarily employed a twist of dry wit to cope with bewildering things, suddenly looked very severe and he said: *I forbid you from . . .*

Now, now, doña Sol tried to say.

Diego turned to Montse, inviting her to act as a witness to this unacceptable behaviour.

I see that the truth hurts, Diego said.

But Montse didn't move. She betrayed no emotion at all. For her, without doubt, don Jaime had been right.

The more time passed, the more Montse realised that when father and son clashed she almost always secretly took don Jaime's side. A subtle kind of mutual sympathy had taken root. Protected by their recent family ties, Montse and don Jaime granted each other a new degree of freedom, a level of trust, something she could never have imagined possible a few months earlier, convinced that her social condition only warranted his scorn and indifference.

One afternoon as they were drinking coffee in the drawing room, don Jaime turned to Montse and gently placed a hand on her arm, a rich person's hand, with white feminine skin, and said, *Montsita, can you light my cigarillo?* The way he said *Montsita*, added to the softness of his hand, was like a soothing ointment (*It didn't take much, did it?* my mother says). From then on, don Jaime only ever used this nickname, a pet name her own father, brother and husband had never dared use, out of embarrassment, coyness or just for fear of appearing too soft. *The Spanish male,* (my mother says) *cannot handle any affectionate words since he thinks they belong exclusively to the world of women. He has a very marked idea of his own virility, a very protruding idea, très protubérante, I might even add. He spends a significant part of his life telling himself he's happy he has a pair of balls and he's going to get the best out of them. It's exhausting. The Spanish male, my dear Lidia, is to be avoided at all costs, I've told you a hundred times before, cent fois.*

Any lingering shyness Montse experienced in don Jaime's presence melted away.

Behind his detachment, she discovered a real feeling for others, a sweetness, a tenderness that Diego both longed for and rebuffed. All you had to do was scratch at the weathered surface a little and the tenderness appeared. It had been pummelled over

186

the years, but it was still there.

Although they never stated it outright, Montse and don Jaime enjoyed each other's company. Theirs was an unfamiliar and joyous complicity, unlike any other, a source of much-needed moral support.

Montse was more able to put up with doña Pura's diatribes against the hordes of Red proletarians destroying the country's infrastructure (*and for what purpose? To sit back and twiddle their thumbs! Yes, señores!*). She could even put up with the endless groans about the aches and pains of the woman's tender Catholic organs.

Don Jaime, who always found an excuse to leave the house and spend his evenings in town with his friend Fabregat, drinking vermouth and soda, now began to enjoy staying in with *his three women*, playing games like a child again: battleships or *loto* with dried chickpeas and beans. He was secretly delighted that the vicissitudes of war, and his son's unorthodox personality, had brought him such a daughter-in-law.

Don Jaime felt as if he'd covertly grown younger and Montse felt as if she'd matured (or *elevated herself* a little, as doña Pura might have put it).

Thanks to don Jaime, Montse learned that courtesy and attentiveness to others do improve human relations and don't necessarily require *effeminate affectation* (as her father maintained) or *bourgeois hypocrisy* (as José maintained). *War*, don Jaime said, *shouldn't turn us into savages.*

The savages, his son immediately replied, *are those who exploit*

187

the poor, and the atmosphere in the house turned sour again.

Thanks to don Jaime too, Montse learned how to dress with style. Since the events of July everyone was taking care to wear the tattiest possible clothes, keeping the same dirty shirt on for days so as not to be suspected of colluding with the enemies of the people. The Reds were particularly conscientious on this score.

Montse learned the meanings of fancy words such as to "felicitate", to "pine", and to "err", words no-one had ever used in front of her, and they made her feel as if her mind had expanded.

She developed a taste for beautiful things: bunches of dahlias on a dining-room table, knives and forks laid out in perfect symmetry, artistic dishes with a sprinkle of parsley on top. Montse kept these tastes all her life. During her exile in France they became her way of resisting (resisting nostalgia, resisting bleakness, but, above all, resisting the poverty she was condemned to by Diego's paltry salary when he only found employment on construction sites in Toulouse).

Don Jaime and Montse frequently burst out laughing for no particular reason, or rather their reason was a heartening realisation they were so dissimilar and yet so alike. *We laughed at the same things, both of us,* my mother tells me, *we shared a sort of philosophical outlook on life, we were cool, as you lot might say nowadays, despite the fact he was at the top of the pecking order and I was really way down below.* Both had seen their worlds collapse: don Jaime the supposedly stable world of ancient traditions, lightly refreshed, but not saved, by a pinch of appropriate easy-going Socialism, and Montse the world of enthralling dreams and young fantasies, but which, like her brother, she now saw crumbling in front of her eyes. Neither Montse nor don Jaime, however, had any nostalgia or self-pity, both almost always chose to be light-hearted, defusing family dramas when they were on the brink of imploding, steering arguments towards politically neutral territory (notably on culinary matters: *Would you like your chickpeas in a salad or in a stew?*), gently mocking Diego's theories in the hope of making him waver; and tackling doña Sol's similarly rigid views – but without much hope of making her relent. *You'd have had more luck talking to a brick wall.*

For the first time in a long while, both Montse and don Jaime could feel a renewed warmth in their hearts, a mutual trust uniting them, a sense of relief, a deep affinity despite their differences. How to explain it without mawkishness? Let's say they believed they had a solid friendship, a strong *amistad* (*the Spanish word for "friendship" has much more panache*, my mother tells me. So be it).

One evening after dinner, when Diego was on duty at the town hall, don Jaime and Montse found themselves alone in the drawing room – doña Sol had retired to her room and doña Pura was already asleep (both had conveniently come down with some ailment).

Montse had long yearned for such a tête-à-tête. Often she'd launched into a sentence in the hope of confessing something to don Jaime, but each time she'd been prevented from carrying on by the untimely arrival of another member of the family.

But on that evening, after serving him a cognac (*Don Jaime always said, "My kingdom for a cognac!" Why my kingdom? I don't know*, my mother adds, *it always struck me as strange*), Montse sat down opposite him and told him bravely, without sounding rude, that she'd taken the comment he'd made at 10.00 on that morning of July 18, 1936 (when she'd come to be interviewed for the job of maid), very badly. *She seems quite humble.* A remark coated with an unbearable trace of contempt. It had wounded her more than the lashes her father subjected her to with his belt. It had, in fact, upset her so much she'd wished there and then for the revolution to come.

Don Jaime was appalled.

Having taken a few seconds to get over the shock, he asked Montse to forgive him for his clumsiness.

Montse at once begged him to forgive her for her sensitivity.

Both mumbled various hurried excuses, exonerations and infinite regrets: *I shouldn't have, sorry, of course not, but frankly, but no, I shouldn't have, but no, but yes*, until they both burst out laughing.

They remained a while in the silence and peace of the drawing room as the night's shadows poured in.

What are you thinking? Don Jaime asked Montse as the silence continued, her eyes contemplating something beyond the window.

Was it because she had dared talk to him of the disastrous moment when they first met, and the anger and shame she'd endured? Or was it because after so many timid and aborted attempts she had finally earned his friendship and trust? Or was it for a different reason altogether? The fact is that Montse dared bring up a subject they had never touched on, apart from the odd word (according to the strange rule that we talk about everything except the things we're dying to say): Diego's early years.

This is what he told her:

At the age of twenty, don Jaime had gone to study law in Barcelona. In those days he read Voltaire and Miguel de Unamuno, and had no time for his mother's bigotry. He advocated Socialism, while milling around with his fellow bourgeois, playing in golf tournaments in the morning and attending workers' meetings in the afternoon. By night he invited his rich friends to drink with him in the bars on barrio Chino.

It was in the Chiringuito bar that he met a waitress named Paloma and fell madly in love with her.

They moved into the apartment don Jaime's father rented for his son and they lived hidden away from the world – in sin, as some people might have said at the time.

Don Jaime had no reason to doubt the various vexations, humiliations and persecutions Paloma began to complain about. He believed her when she said she was being closely observed by the neighbour on the landing, a blonde with an impatient, wriggly arse (a prick-tease, basically). He believed her when she said this neighbour had her eye on her for some obscure and threatening reason and that she liked to bad-mouth her at the first available opportunity, going so far as to tell the other residents of the building that Paloma was a woman of loose morals.

He trusted Paloma despite all evidence to the contrary, for the simple reason that he loved her.

He said he'd put the vile blonde in her place, demand that she put a stop to her machinations and explain herself. *What did she want with Paloma? Why was she spying on her? And why was she spreading such horrible rumours?*

He believed Paloma right up to the day he found her standing in the kitchen, listening at the wall, a hunted look on her face.

I can feel her.

Who?

The neighbour.

Through the wall?

I can feel her.

That's not possible.

You don't believe me? Why? Are you on her side? Are you in this together?

Don Jaime was thrown by Paloma's behaviour. It was abnormal, strange, alarming, pathological even. After a few moments of doubt, and some anguished thoughts, he came to the conclusion that she was delirious. Paloma, for her part, believed she had a sixth sense. She'd spent recent months spying on the noises coming from the apartment next door. *I can hear the coded sounds coming through the wall*, she said with a shudder: troubling messages, indecipherable signals. The blonde neighbour was secretly trying to get in contact with don Jaime. It was clear to her now: her lover had the hots for *the other one* (that's what she called the neighbour, *the other one, the bitch, the whore, the cockroach). You'd have to be blind not to see it.*

Paloma banged on the wall three times, shouted at don Jaime, a deranged look in her eyes. *What are you waiting for? Go and fuck her. She turns you on, doesn't she? Admit it.*

Don't be ridiculous, don Jaime told her. He tried to explain the absurdity of her accusations, to analyse the situation logically.

Paloma wouldn't stop. *Go! Go to her! What are you waiting for? Leave! Go now!*

She began to scream desperately, punching him, insulting him, and all don Jaime could think was that he had to get out of there and stay out of there for good, stay single, alone, alone, alone.

But Paloma very soon announced she was pregnant. Don Jaime found himself hoping their child might bring an end to her derangement. Diego was born on June 12, 1917. Paloma's hallucinations only got worse.

For two years, Diego and his mother lived anchored to one another, inseparable, indistinguishable. So much so that don Jaime felt that he was an intruder, an outsider who might at any moment burst their idyllic bubble with his big feet. They survived thanks to the money he provided and he ended up moving into a room of his own and studying law without much enthusiasm.

Paloma's behaviour became more and more erratic, fed by the hallucinatory feeling that her neighbour was persecuting her. It was as if her own spirit were torturing her more cruelly than if she'd been in hell itself. Believing herself to be the victim of an evil spell and in danger of imminent death, Paloma barged her way into the neighbour's apartment brandishing a pair of scissors and threatened to poke the woman's eyes out. There were screams, the sound of fighting, running footsteps. The neighbours rushed to see. The police pitched up. Paloma was led to the police station with a weeping Diego in her arms. She was put away in a psychiatric hospital with the mysterious diagnosis of "Capgras delusional disorder".

Don Jaime was desperate. He was recommended a family he could entrust Diego to – what today might be called a foster family. But they did not do much fostering.

The Fuentes fed, washed and dressed the child and took him to school. In that respect they were above criticism.

They taught him to say *Thank you*, and *After you, please*, *Buenos días* in the morning and *Adiós* when leaving, to stand up straight, to wipe his feet, to eat with his mouth shut, not to answer back, especially to adults, and above all, not to ask too many questions.

When little Diego challenged their orders and asked them about important issues, about death and abandonment, the kind of things that trouble children, he was told to shut up. The Fuentes were above reproach in every other way. They were just keen to teach him good manners: no questions, no lies.

If Diego asked how long his mother would be ill, *ten days, twenty days, a hundred days?* (he knew how to count to a hundred already), they told him to go back and look at his school books again rather than worry about such trivial matters.

When don Jaime visited – twice a month – the Fuentes went out of their way to tell him about the delicious food they were giving his child, the expensive clothes they bought him, how they were doing their best, day after day, to build up his strength.

Although he was fed, dressed and generally brushed and polished (as I said, the Fuentes really couldn't be criticised), the child sensed that something was missing. He was filled with distress without knowing its cause.

You can't get any sadder than that, I say.

Perfectement, my mother agrees, *and I forbid you from joking about this*.

It was when Diego was alone in bed, feeling vulnerable, the shadows of the night creeping in – without a loving word from anyone, without a kind gesture or a smile – that despair overwhelmed him and twisted itself into terrifying shapes. He cried out for help and wept, not understanding what he was frightened of, though he knew he was frightened to death, and his fear stirred up the most awful thoughts (he never lost this feeling of fear and towards the end his days it crushed him, landing him in a psychiatric hospital just like his mother).

Señora Fuentes would calmly walk to Diego's room and ask him, in her own faultless way, what the matter was, telling him not to cry too loudly as he was going to wake everyone else up.

If he carried on crying, señor Fuentes allowed him to keep his bedside lamp on.

And if he still carried on sobbing after that, señor Fuentes, in his own faultless way, went back to the room and told the boy that crybabies were, in his opinion, the most pitiful type of human being.

So Diego came to repress his emotions in front of his *tía* and *tío*, as he called the Fuentes, all of his emotions in fact, a form of restriction men don't normally impose on themselves until later in life. He learned to grit his teeth and not to mention his sufferings, not let on how much he hurt. His face became unusually hard for a boy his age. He had the sort of expression you see in children who have escaped from conflict zones. It ripped his father's heart in two every time he came to see Diego.

When don Jaime was alone with the boy, he would ask him anxiously: *Are you alright, my little Dieguito? Are you sad? You have to tell your papa if something's wrong. You have to tell your papa everything.*

Diego would just shake his head and say everything was alright, for the good reason that he was not able to understand what was wrong.

Yet, when it came to saying goodbye, the child clung to his father's legs to prevent him from leaving, *Don't go, don't go, don't go.* Don Jaime, on the verge of tears himself, had to prise his son's fingers off him. The child's grip was staggeringly strong – he had to be brutal, even though he was about to leave the boy for another two weeks. Don Jaime wanted to take the child with him, but each time he abandoned the idea as he tried to imagine how he'd manage looking after a child on his own.

As soon as don Jaime married doña Sol he went and fetched Diego and brought him home. He was seven years old.

Bernanos counted up the dead on the island of Majorca: three thousand murders committed over the first seven months of the war, which is to say a rate of nearly fifteen executions a day for a period of about two hundred and ten days.

With extreme sarcasm, Bernanos calculated that the island could be crossed from one end to the other in two hours. A watchful driver, therefore, might be able to encounter up to fifteen smashed-in, deviant skulls in one day, an impressive score.

With the very air of Majorca so saturated with horrors of every kind, how could its beautiful almond trees ever flower again?

On March 28, 1937, Montse gave birth to a little girl.

So many things had happened in the village since the outbreak of war that no-one noticed Montse's supposedly premature baby weighed a plump 3.82 kilogrammes and was as healthy as anything.

She was named Lunita.

Lunita is my older sister. She is seventy-three now. I was born ten years later. Diego, my father, was her stepfather, her fake father.

Lunita charmed everyone from the moment she was born.

Doña Pura was over the moon, excessive in her affections. She didn't seem to mind that her dignity took a bit of a battering. As soon as Lunita cried, she took the baby in her bony arms and put on silly voices and with an idiotically smily face would say: *I'm going to go pat pat on your botty*. A little botty she sprinkled with talcum powder as if it were a *pâtisserie* and which she then pretended to eat with ecstatic kisses, singing, *How sweet, how pretty, how beautiful you are, my little darling, my treasure, my love, Qué mona, qué linda, qué hermosa eres, cariño mío, tesoro mío, amor mío, and so on and so on.*

Doña Sol was equally gaga and put the child on her lap to make her gallop up and down to the rhythm of *Giddy-up, little donkey, giddy-up, go, go, go,* with Lunita giggling and chortling away.

Diego had wanted a boy and was hard put to hide his disappointment on the day of the birth. He stared at Lunita's crumpled little face with a sort of sad disbelief. Yet he lovingly fed her bottles of milk, lovingly waited for her to burp: the most charming, the most subtle, the most lyrical, spiritual and musical burp in the world. He congratulated her for her artistic grace, then hugged her in all sorts of dotty ways, *give me a smile, my sweetie pie, a little giggle for your papa.* As for Montse, she was overjoyed to see her daughter flourishing. She seemed so lively and so full of character, and wilful despite her sweet airs. Montse couldn't help but believe that the revolution of 1936 had had an unexpected result already: it had radically altered her family's genetic make-up. Nothing in Lunita's face suggested that expression of humility transmitted from generation to generation like a dominant gene in her bloodline, a recurring call for humiliation.

What a character, don Jaime said, amazed at how the small child sometimes shuddered with rage and refused her bottle.

Lunita became the central fact of Montse's life, everything else was secondary. She scarcely paid attention when an ashen-faced Diego came to tell her that the inhabitants of Guernica had been relentlessly bombarded by the planes of the Cóndor division. She was too excited by the possibility she might have heard her adored one-month-old baby utter the word "*pipi*". If true, she said in all seriousness, the child could turn out to be of exceptional intelligence.

Montse was crazy about her baby. She'd never been fond of her husband's redheadedness, but now the purely coincidental hints of auburn in Lunita's hair charmed her. *You're my little red squirrel*, she whispered, *my little fox, my little red hen, my red-haired girl, my otter, my carrot top, my caramelo.*

And she sang:

> *Dice la gente que tiene*
> *Veinticuatro horas al día.*
> *Si tuviera veintisiete*
> *Tres horas más te querría.*

> *People say they have twenty-four hours a day.*
> *But if I had twenty-seven*
> *There'd be three more hours of love and play.*

José fell under the spell of Lunita's charm, and his sadness seemed to fade when he was with her. Montse persuaded him to be the girl's non-religious godfather, and he agreed to visit the Burgos house provided that Diego was out. He took his role very seriously: he rocked the child while singing the "Internationale", told her stories in which Makhno and Lacenaire were the heroes and, between cuddles, kept the baby up to scratch with the most recent anti-Franco speeches. Tiny Lunita gurgled happily, while doña Pura retreated to her room aghast.

The whole family had gone totally gaga.

They were not so very perturbed when talk of baptising the little girl began. Doña Sol and doña Pura believed Lunita should be christened immediately lest she spend eternity walking alone in purgatorial limbo, and set about locating a surviving priest. Diego declared himself resolutely against such a farce.

Don Jaime agreed to go along with the parents' decision.

José threatened all-out chaos if his adored niece was brainwashed before she so much as knew how to speak.

Unsure of what to do, Montse asked for more time to make up her mind.

On March 19, 1937, nine days before Lunita's birth, Pope Pius XI published his encyclical, *DIVINI REDEMPTORIS*, to warn of an *intrinsically perverse danger threatening the world* (to quote the holy man).

This danger, this *satanic scourge* (to quote the holy man again), was none other than atheistic Bolshevik Communism, expressly designed to overturn social order and suck the essence out of Christian family life.

Communism professed, amongst other aberrations, the prin- ciple of women's emancipation, and (to quote the holy man once more) suggested: *removing women from the family and the care of children, to be thrust instead into public life and collective production* – where bacteria and nefarious influences of all sorts surely awaited them.

But the greatest danger by far lay in the fact that a human society founded on Bolshevik materialistic principles could not, evidently, offer any values other than those of the economic system. Had His Holiness the Pope, too absorbed by his love of God, inadvertently and regrettably muddled up Communist and Capitalist economic models? Most likely.

To do him justice, it should be pointed out that in February 1939, Pius XI, with habitual Vatican adeptness, also undertook the drafting of another encyclical denouncing Nazi persecutions and the Italian Fascists' manipulations of the Church. But he died the night before it was published.

On May 3, 1937, José heard on the radio that a group of assailants, acting on the Communists' behalf (as if to prove His Holiness Pius XI right), had burst into the headquarters of a city held by the Anarchists and the P.O.U.M. and set about exterminating the whole lot of them once and for all.

After several days of fighting, the Communist militia managed to either arrest, imprison or kill a large number of Anarchists and P.O.U.M members, accusing them of being turncoats covertly working for Hitler. (Ilya Ehrenburg, when he wrote *No Pasarán*, endorsed this accusation, but the book, strangely, later disappeared from his official oeuvre.)

The Communists had long wanted to control the political game and excise mention of the Anarchist movement from its account of the revolution. They had done their best, to discredit Anarchism by slandering and spreading rumours. Slandering, though, was a sissy's method. They were going to have to get serious at some point. How? By killing, of course. And that's exactly what they did.

José felt desperate.

He would be yet more desperate a month later when he learned that the Anarchists had been violently crushed and excluded from the regional government, the P.O.U.M. dissolved and its militants arrested. Their leader Andrés Nin – who had taken the ill-advised step of publicly denouncing the Moscow Trials – was tortured and assassinated in an operation ordered by Stalin with the complicity of the Spanish government. (*Stalin is the noon, the maturity of man and the peoples. Stalinists, let us bear this title with pride*, Neruda wrote. *The most servile and Stalinist of poets*, José used to say – according to my mother.)

To cap it all, in August 1937, hundreds of collectivised communes were broken up by armed forces under Communist command.

None of this got a mention in the European press at the time.

It is worth noting, however, that on December 17, 1936, *Pravda* had given some prior warning: *The purging of Trotskyist and Anarchist–Unionist elements has begun and the task will be carried out with the same vigour as it was in the Soviet Union.*

José found out about these events, the *Hechos de Mayo* (as they came to be known), through the Anarchist radio station he listened to every morning.

He felt his anger erupting when he heard the news and ran straight to the town hall. He was a man possessed, his legs propelled by his fury. He looked at no-one on his way, he didn't notice a thing, all he could feel was the blood banging away at his temples, his feet pounding the ground, his body pulsating. He burst into Diego's office, livid, breathless, his hair dishevelled, his heart out of control, suffocating with rage. He didn't seem to notice that four young assistants were already talking to Diego. He saw nothing, heard nothing, noticed nothing. He had no thoughts, just an urge to kill.

He stood right in front of Diego, staring into his eyes, and yelled, *You are nothing but a bastard traitor.*

As Diego just looked at him coldly, without saying a thing, he yelled again: *Try and deny your friends had nothing to do with yesterday's events!*

Please explain what you mean, Diego said, without flinching, his voice calm, detached, monotonous, although he'd understood perfectly well.

You're nothing but a filthy traitor, José shrieked, *you disgust me.*

Watch what you're saying, Diego threatened, quietly, stressing each word, without raising his voice. *You could regret it.*

The two men looked each other up and down.

If you weren't Montse's brother, I'd . . .

Diego didn't finish his sentence.

Seven months later, when the drama between Diego and José was being commented on by all and sundry, two of the young assistants present that day remembered the way Diego uttered his threat, and the premonition it seemed to carry.

Don't you ever mention my sister's name in front of me again, José yelled, storming out of the office without noticing the assistants' appalled expressions. He raced down the calle del Sepulcro, oblivious to the reactions of people coming the other way, all of them alarmed by José's wild and maddened scowl. He charged home, heedless of his mother's panic as she waited for him at the top of the steps – he shoved her to one side so angrily she almost fell.

After José had stamped out of the town hall, leaving his brother-in-law with just a slight quiver at the corner of his mouth, Diego asked his assistants to give him sometime alone: he needed to think. Since his marriage to Montse, he had vaguely entertained the idea of trying to win José over to his political cause. He had believed his brother-in-law's rebelliousness was like a mild fever that could be cured. Indeed, all rebellion could be cured. A nice lime-flower tisane, a kiss on the scratched knee or a kick up the arse, and home to Mamá. No, not at all. He had been wrong. This was different. In José's case his rebellion was a commitment, a commitment beyond his will, beyond reason, something irrepressible, as dangerous and demanding as love. It drew on his blood, every drop of it . . .

Diego was sure of one thing: the rift between the two of them could no longer be repaired. In a way, and although he found it difficult to admit, this was a release. It freed him from José's endless disapproval, from his mockery, from his rejection of the most unquestionable dogmas. It freed him, above all, from

José's hellish, inexhaustible, incurable purity.

Perhaps it delivered him, too, from the old childhood jealousy still weighing on his heart. Strangely, since his marriage to Montse, this old childhood jealousy, which he'd managed more or less to conceal under political differences, had continued to grow. He couldn't rid himself of the thought that José was kinder than he was, more seductive, more hypnotic, more Spanish even, that he possessed something both mysterious and almost feminine called charm, and that if his wife were to compare the two of them, he would come out second best.

Some claimed this jealousy, this wound of Diego's, this inadequacy he saw in himself, as opposed to the grace he envied in José, was partly responsible for the drama that soon unfolded and brought their intertwined destinies to such a fatal conclusion.

Je t'aime, my mother says, taking my hand.

In July 1937, the bishops and archbishops of Spain issued a collective letter.

Its aim was to express overwhelming approval for Franco's leadership and to show the clergy's determination to muster God's forces in the battle against evil.

The signatories were:

✠ ISIDRO CARD. GOMÁ Y TOMAS, Archbishop of
Toledo

✠ EUSTAQUIO CARD. ILUNDAIN Y ESTEBAN,
Archbishop of Seville

✝ PRUDENCIO, Archbishop of Valencia

✝ MANUEL, Archbishop of Burgos

✝ RIGOBERTO, Archbishop of Zaragoza

✝ TOMÁS, Archbishop of Santiago

✝ AGUSTÍN, Archbishop of Granada, Apostolic
    Administrator of Almería, Guadix, and Jaén

✝ JOSÉ, Archbishop-Bishop of Majorca

✝ ADOLFO, Bishop of Córdoba, Apostolic Administrator
    of the Bishopric and Priorship of Ciudad Real

✝ ANTONIO, Bishop of Astorga

✝ LEOPOLDO, Bishop of Madrid-Alcalá

✝ MANUEL, Bishop of Palencia

✝ ENRIQUE, Bishop of Salamanca

✝ VALENTIN, Bishop of Solsona

✝ JUSTINO, Bishop of Urgel

✝ MIGUEL DE LOS SANTOS, Bishop of Cartagena

✝ FIDEL, Bishop of Calahorra

✝ FLORENCIO, Bishop of Orense

✝ RAFAEL, Bishop of Lugo

✝ FELIX, Bishop of Tortosa

✝ FR. ALBINO, Bishop of Tenerife

✝ JUAN, Bishop of Jaca

✝ JUAN, Bishop of Vich

✝ NICANOR, Bishop of Tarazona, Apostolic Administrator
    of Tudela

✝ JOSÉ, Bishop of Santander

✠ FELICIANO, Bishop of Plasencia

✠ ANTONIO, Bishop of Quersoneso de Creta, Apostolic
Administrator of Ibiza

✠ LUCIANO, Bishop of Segovia

✠ MANUEL, Bishop of Curio, Apostolic Administrator
of Ciudad Rodrigo

✠ MANUEL, Bishop of Zamora

✠ LINO, Bishop of Huesca

✠ ANTONIO, Bishop of Tuy

✠ JOSÉ MARIA, Bishop of Badajoz

✠ JOSÉ, Bishop of Gerona

✠ JUSTO, Bishop of Oviedo

✠ FR. FRANCISCO, Bishop of Coria

✠ BENJAMÍN, Bishop of Mondoñedo

✠ TOMÁS, Bishop of Osma

✠ FR. ANSELMO, Bishop of Teruel-Albarracín

✠ SANTOS, Bishop of Avila

✠ BALBINO, Bishop of Málaga

✠ MARCELINO, Bishop of Pamplona

✠ ANTONIO, Bishop of the Canaries

✠ HILARIO YABEN, Vicar Capitular of Sigüenza

✠ EUGENIO DOMAICA, Vicar Capitular of Cádiz

✠ EMILIO F. GARCIA, Vicar Capitular of Ceuta

✠ FERNANDO ÁLVAREZ, Vicar Capitular of León

✠ JOSÉ ZURITA, Vicar Capitular of Valladolid

*

The priests of Spain, the majority of them simple men, out of touch with the centres of power and close to the common people, had to go along with the basic principles of this letter of unconditional support for Franco whether they liked it or not. They had to shroud their consciences with their cassocks, and many ended up paying for it with their lives.

In a French newspaper on August 27, 1937, the author Paul Claudel unhesitatingly approved the collective letter. He had previously voiced his heartfelt support for Franco and his sublime crusade. How a person like Franco managed to have so many illustrious supporters seemed abhorrent to Bernanos. "I would probably never have written about Franco had you not attempted to turn this nightmarish tinpot dictator into a kind of Christian hero for the French public ... Why on earth should I be expected to admire a general who has turned his legitimacy into a ferocious ideal to better hide his double-crossing?"

Claudel approved the collective letter in the same way he began to hate Jews and claim that the greatest threat to France came from its striking workers rather than from Hitler or Mussolini.

Some were persuaded by such arguments. Not Bernanos. "If we are to believe some right-minded people," he wrote, "satisfied French workers are dying of happiness and well-being." And he went on to remind his readers of the abominable living conditions of the poor in France.

Bernanos had understood the method. By barking at the French working class, Claudel, and others like him, were trying to drown out the clamour of the battalions goose-stepping to the tune of Europe's two dictators. He refused to be part of any attempt to make the workers of France responsible for the failures of an entire country.

Had the revolution died before it had even begun? José wondered as he watched his black mule turn the waterwheel round and round. Should I be mourning the life I dreamed of in Lérida? Is this what maturity is? Is it just defeat?

Diego's tireless repetition of Communist propaganda about the Anarchists being allies of Franco by default had finally bedded itself in the villagers' minds. José continued to slide downwards in their esteem, until he became an object of general disapproval. A pariah.

The small landowners condemned him in the name of land ownership (which he had wanted to abolish); the day labourers condemned him in the name of organised labour (which he had questioned); the devout condemned him in the name of religion (he had blasphemed by painting the Virgin Mary's crown red); the prigs of both sexes (who found his eclectic swear words and his overall catalogue of curses highly offensive) condemned him in the name of decency; and Diego, of course, condemned him in the name of their ancient childhood hatred (expediently transformed into political rivalry).

At first, José's reaction was as logical as paradoxical. The more violently people disparaged his Anarchist utopia the more vigorously he upheld it.

He vowed that nothing would make him change his mind, ever.

His utopia was a quivering glow of hope at the bottom of a well, a generous breath of air in a world full of cockroaches. He said that the idea of change, even if he'd only entertained it for a short while, had altered him for ever, turned him into another person. He maintained that Spain was the only country in which the dream could still flourish. On days when he was particularly inspired, he said his dream was like a plant buried for millennia but whose seeds still had the ability to flower. *Let the dogs obey Diego, I'm going to follow my dream!* he hurled at his mother, who looked at him with more and more bewilderment as the days went by.

Then, little by little, his faith began to stumble and teeter. His disillusionment grew. Or rather, he went through a period when he could neither fully believe in his dream nor give up on it. He began to say that, in essence, people being what they were – imperfect in every way, very imperfect in fact – and society being subject to their changeable desires and fantasies, what he now espoused was the idea of a wise utopia stripped of all naivety, a utopia as red as blood, as black as the human soul, an informed utopia, clear-sighted, cleansed of misty illusions, something impossible, unattainable . . . but everyone still had to yearn for it, without delay, because it would lead to emancipation of the loftiest kind. Such was his new vision.

But something in him had broken. His eloquence could no longer paper over the cracks. The sorrow he'd experienced in the café on las Ramblas, the time he'd overheard the men from his own side boasting about their hatred, the sorrow he'd managed to keep at arm's length for a while, now returned and engulfed him. Bitterness appeared in its wake. *It was always going to end badly*, José said, *it was a foregone conclusion. I've worked for nothing*, he said, *that'll teach me. Dreams are a waste of time, a bloody waste of time.*

José, the consummate dreamer, had at last lost his dream. He slipped into mourning. It was grief for his rebellious spirit, for his childhood, for his innocence. And Diego alone was to blame, for all of it.

Diego became his *idée fixe.*

His perfect enemy.

After the *Hechos de Mayo*, the events of May, he hated him more fiercely. Diego had become yet more abhorrent, yet more inexcusable.

José directed all his contempt at him.

He said a hundred times a day that Diego, *that dog*, had betrayed the revolution. José spoke of the revolution as others might speak of a lover. It was exactly what the revolution was to him. *That dog* had sullied the revolution. He'd debased it. He'd forced it to commit suicide. He had shat on it while pretending to serve it. He had not understood that before claiming to be part of a revolution you have to make it a part of yourself. He explained this to his sighing mother, who listened with terrified resignation. He demonstrated what he meant to Maruca, the grocer's wife, who listened to him in the way an adult listens to a child's prattling, and for the hundredth time he proved his point to Juan who led him to Bendición's café to distract him.

A vermouth, José ordered.

Make that two, Juan said.

Talk in the café was all about the harvest and the quantity of olives the trees were expected to give.

It's the only thing that interests them, José said.

Olives, and sex, Juan corrected him.

And the Virgin Mary, José said.

It all goes together, Juan said.

After which they fell into a depressed silence.

And Rosita? José suddenly asked.

What about her?

Is she still working in the school canteen?

Of course she is, Juan laughed. *What do you think she's doing, having a wild time in Paris?*

Then they fell into another depressed silence.

Look at all these cretins, José shouted. This was his mystical moment. *Human beings*, he said, frowning, *are now just out to cheat one another and lie, more and more. It's a form of progress, I suppose, but in reverse – they enjoy getting swindled, they're won over by the first person to come along and shout louder than the rest, the first who hollers: Follow the leader. They're all cowards, crawlers, waiting to be enslaved, and servile fear has replaced their moral codes. They get over the death of their wife or husband quicker than the loss of their house or goat, I've seen it hundreds of times. It's an understatement to say they're cowards, and what they call mala suerte, bad luck, is nothing but the name they give their cowardice.*

They're weak and vindictive because of it, they're ....
....
....
....
....
....
....
....
....
....
.... and so on and
so forth, the litany of human depths and failures had no end.
José listed them gloomily for hour after hour at the bar while an
equally gloomy Juan ordered yet another vermouth, *por favor*.
The poor man was in urgent and constant need of a boost of
some kind.

José then entered a new phase. He took to blaming himself. And
the violence he employed to do so frightened everyone, particularly his mother.

He cursed himself. Berated himself. Hated himself.

He wanted to vomit up everything he had once loved.

He wished he could disassociate himself from the things he'd
once been.

He'd been a fool, he said, *to believe he'd found paradise, but
it was a paradise for puppets and lapdogs. As for Purity, Eternal*

Youth, the Land of Milk and Honey, Fraternal Love, all those exalted aspirations, they were all claptrap. They were cages for suckers, pitiful consolations invented by losers like him who'd been wounded by the world and sought protection in fantasies.

He had to cleanse himself of all this. Quickly. Without tears.

He had to destroy his castles in the air, hide the sickly sentimentality of it all.

He burrowed his way into a tunnel of wretched thoughts, showering everything around him with the cinders of his mourning. He said Spain was heading for disaster. The end was upon them. *Everything is over, fucked, jodido, I'm not waiting or hoping for anything else. I don't give a damn about the village, don't give a damn about anything, don't give a damn.*

He had previously proclaimed, with a certain panache, that it was better to be a dead lion than a living dog, but now he too started to whine that he was living like a dog.

But am I even alive? he wondered.

He grew bitter.

A wrinkle, a furrow of sourness, appeared at the corner of his mouth.

His irascibility got worse and he appeared to enjoy torturing his mother. He offended her, wounded her with his words. He was constantly exasperated by her.

He kicked dogs in the belly as they sauntered past him. He flew into a rage at the smallest thing.

It seemed as if he were looking for something irrecoverable, something final.

In the village they said he'd become a bore. *He goes on and on. He needs to change his tune.*

He kept himself to himself. His darkness scared everyone. He became someone to avoid.

People belittled him.

They said he was a bad loser.

They listed his weaknesses.

They barely returned his greetings.

Told you so, they said. *See where his grand ideas got him. They've made him crazy.*

The exaggerated rumours, the same ones that had been spread about José at the start of the summer, swung back into fashion again. Everyone was criticising him. They were all at it. Even those who didn't really care, since they were eager to prove they hadn't been fooled by him either.

They delighted in his downfall.

Diego more than anyone. He watched José fall the way others stop and stare at car crashes or attend public executions.

Come the beginning of December 1937, another rumour was gaining ground (one of don Jaime's employees had foolishly spread the word). It was being said that a small group of Falangists, led by the foreman El Perrito, was planning to take the town hall by force.

Diego's first concern was to inform the regional authorities, who promised him two vehicles and some reinforcements to crush any attack. As soon as they got wind of this, José and Juan understood that it was their one and only chance to pull themselves out of their pit of depression, the perfect occasion to put an end to their apathy and stupor (which they were starting to get used to). They had been listless for months, unproductive, filled with resentment, spouting nasty comments to distract themselves, testing out their sarcastic, uncharacteristic snickering, refusing all interaction with their village peers, who, so they said, lived and thought like pigs. Patently not everyone had their talent for despair.

The prospect of a fight brought them unexpected relief. They were going to battle it out. Things were going to get messy. People would see what they were made of. They had a soaring yearning for heroism, though it might have been for distress too.

They told Diego they were ready to join forces with him. They'd be there to back him up on the day. It was time they overcame their differences and proved they were all up to the challenges at hand.

Diego had no choice but to accept.

Without any consultation between the various parties, they all threw themselves into this act of bravado, though common sense might have dictated a different course of action.

To this day, no-one can say precisely how events unfolded. Accounts are contradictory, confusing, fragmented. Bit by bit, the following facts emerged: on December 16, the Falangists, led by El Perrito, set up some sort of heavy artillery behind El Peque's house. It is not known where they got their weapons from, but the small group was made up of five of don Jaime's own farm labourers – men who were deeply attached to him, who respected him like a medieval lord. The foreman had no difficulty, therefore, in persuading the labourers of the legitimacy of the attack as it was designed to wrest power from the renegade son. It was living Shakespeare. The foreman, it should be noted, had cooked up this plan on his own, without mentioning a word of it to don Jaime, despite what some ill-intentioned people suggested afterwards.

José and Juan positioned themselves as lookouts on high ground, next to the fields belonging to the Murcia family. They crouched in the grass, behind a low wall, armed with hunting rifles, nervously waiting for the arrival of the commando reinforcements.

Diego and the four young Communists who usually escorted him had taken up positions behind the Aznars' house. They were all armed with guns, grenades hanging from their belts, ready to surround El Peque's house where the Falangists lay in wait.

Fighting broke out when the reinforcements reached the Falangists' lair. At that moment José and Juan, and the small group led by Diego, rushed forward.

They said there were shouts and screams, a skirmish and a wave of panic. Shells fell, guns were fired in all directions, along with orders and counter-orders. Thick smoke prevented anyone from seeing who was shooting at whom. Confusion reigned.

Six men lay dead.

The foreman and two of his men were taken prisoner.

Juan, Diego and three of his assistants survived unscathed.

The commando reinforcements left the scene unharmed.

José was hit in the chest. It was never established who shot him. Thrown to the ground, he felt for the painless gash near his heart, looked at his bloodied fingers, and muttered desperately, *What have they done to me?* He tried to move his legs, but they would not budge. He wanted to shout out to Juan for help, but he had no strength left in his voice. Instead he tried to dredge up images he loved, but none came. He heard explosions, short bursts of gunfire, cries of pain, swearing, the far-off whining of a dog. Then the sound of gunshots faded, all noise gently died down, and he felt himself sliding into a dull, saturating warmth. He stared at the immenseness of the sky. He had no hand to hold on to. There was no loving face looking down on him. He remained *alone, utterly alone, solito* (my mother wipes the corner of an eye at this point).

When the gunshots had finished, Diego went in search of José, calling out his name several times, anguish taking hold of him. He discovered his brother-in-law sprawled out and motionless on the cold ground.

He leaned over his body, placing an arm under his head and tilted it forward. He lay his head back down again. Nothing could be done.

As he walked home, Diego thought briefly about hiding José's death from his wife.

He opened the door.

He was ashen-faced.

Montse immediately understood something terrible had happened.

What's wrong?

Diego said nothing.

She asked him again, her agitation growing.

As Diego still said nothing, she said in an empty voice: *My brother* ...

Diego said *yes* without looking at her.

She leaned against the wall to stop herself from falling.

José was buried three days later with all the villagers following the funeral procession. Whereas a few days previously they had been calling him a brainless dreamer (unrealistic and unhinged), his death led to unanimous feelings of regret accompanied by a wide range of moans and groans. José quickly became the late-lamented José.

Montse sank into a chasm of pain, a pain so immense she seemed both absent and numb, and so numb she no longer bothered reacting to the endlessly negative news from the war-front. She didn't even bother smiling back at Lunita or responding to the affectionate gestures of those around her.

She stopped visiting her mother, who wailed non-stop, *if only José were here to eat the figs, if only he were here for this, if only he were here for that*, weeping her sadness at every possible occasion, all to her neighbours' relish.

Montse stopped humming Carlos Gardel and Juanito Valderrama songs, and spent her days lying flat on her bed. She stopped asking anything of her husband and her face became altogether indecipherable the moment anyone talked about the "event".

Montse's pain was boundless. It turned to a form of madness when Rosita reported the rumour circulating in the village: Diego had killed her brother.

The villagers were better informed about the enmity between the two young men than one might have imagined. By some obscure means, they always ended up finding out snippets of the most hidden and confidential information, constructing preposterous tales from them, which they ended up believing.

The "event" in December unleashed a torrent of new stories, matched by a deep-rooted desire to find culprits for everything. Diego had been singled out as José's murderer and without an iota of proof.

This slandering drove Montse even madder with pain and tipped Diego into such depths of despair that he blamed himself for his carelessness (having initially denied it) in leading the young men to their deaths.

He drank more and more.

Every night, before going to bed, he got into the habit of swigging plum brandy in such quantities that he would collapse on the bed and fall asleep immediately, snoring and snuffling like a pig. Sometimes, before going to sleep, he was overcome by an urge to make love to his wife. He begged her, but she refused. He pinned her arms down. *Leave me, please*, she said, but he continued to crush her with his weight. She wriggled, rocking her head from side to side. He tried to part her thighs with his knees. She kept her legs tightly closed. She said, *Don't touch me, don't touch me or I'll scream.* He breathed his brandy breath over her face. She struggled like a wild animal, he whispered, *I love you, baby, te quiero nena,* in a whiny, feeble drunken voice. She shoved him away in disgust, kicking out of his grasp. Then she shouted, as if wanting to wake up the entire house, *Stop! Stop! Stop!* and ended up fleeing, hiding in the next-door bedroom, double-locking the door.

Diego flopped into a brutish sleep, but woke in a sweat, turned to Montse's side of the bed and groped around for her, but she was gone. He got up, his head heavy, the bedroom floor wobbling. He lurched from side to side. The moment he was up and awake, his pain returned unabated, his remorse with it. And it assailed him just as violently as the night before. He fended it off with another recitation of the same justifications, over and over. Even if he had once longed to drive José as far away from the village as possible, even if his presence had seemed to be a permanent provocation and his face a constant accusation, and even if he had watched his downfall with a dark, unspeakable satisfaction, never, never, never had he wished for his death – that was what he told himself.

One day, as he was reluctantly heading to the town hall, he decided instead to visit Bendición's café.

They all fell quiet the moment he entered.

He wanted to turn and leave immediately, but refused to show it.

He ordered an anisette, knocked it back in one, nodded at the

221

old men playing dominoes, then walked back across the hostile, silent room.

He returned home, troubled to see that his relationship with the villagers was now irrevocably broken. One of his young assistants confirmed this: people were now saying, sharing little knowing winks with one another, that the town hall had turned ginger with rust and depravity.

So Diego changed.

He had always been fussy about his appearance, impeccably dressed, but now he gave up caring. He left his jacket open, pockets gaping, shirt untucked. *He looks like a tramp*, doña Pura said.

His faith in his previous political convictions began to waver too.

José's corpse weighed on his mind, making him look at things differently. He understood how José might have been right to reject the Communist Party line he had so rigorously espoused. As for Anarchist ideals (a form of forbidden fruit for him), they released a slow poison of doubt into him, a doubt that grew and grew. What was there to hold on to if everything else faltered? Who could be trusted? What models, what systems? How could he carry on the fight?

Diego's responsibilities in the village, once such a source of pride, were now a burden. He almost had to drag himself to the town hall. Political matters produced a kind of disgust in him. He considered abandoning his duties, and found himself wishing the war would end, for better or worse, so he could be rid of his obligations.

He aged overnight.

He was only twenty, he looked thirty.

Paranoiac fears started to creep into his unquiet mind during this period. Believing he was being made to feel guilty, although not accused outright by his own family, but definitely blamed, he began to imagine that his father despised him and Montse held him in contempt. He considered blowing his brains out to clear his name.

He had always been so suspicious of everyone, indeed suspicion was one of the most striking traits of his character, and he came to think all the villagers had it in for him, that they were hatching plots against him.

He thought people were staring at him, were up to things behind his back, conspiring to find ways to harm him.

It made him even more jumpy and he locked himself away in his office, the door bolted. At the slightest noise he sat up and reached for the revolver hanging from his belt.

He was more or less able to cope when the Civil War seemed to justify these conspiratorial threats. It was only years later, having emigrated to France, that he succumbed to a persecution complex which twice required him to be interned in a psychiatric hospital.

Don Jaime also changed.

The conduct of the Nationalists in their newly conquered cities sickened him. He found his family insufferable. His son was a great worry to him. Montse's heartbreak was unbearable.

Only the farmers of the village cheered him up, and many sought out his company in the hope of benefiting from his largesse at some point in the future. He neglected his lands, and delegated their management to a young man named Firmín. He spent most of the day in Bendición's café playing dominoes with other men of his age – which was perhaps why he steadily developed a pot belly.

Over the following months, the village's capacity for violence, which until then had only revealed itself through banal, gossipy allegations and a few heated arguments, was brutally reignited. It had little to do with the cycle of the moon.

The villagers were on their guard.

Anyone was a potential enemy.

No-one ventured out into the street without first checking the surrounding area for fear of lurking gunmen.

No-one could rule out the possibility of acts of extreme violence, or ambushes by any number of fanatics.

Above all, people dreaded another assault as tragic as the one that had killed José.

Everyone was frightened of everyone else.

Hearts were filled with resentment and mistrust.

Hatred too.

The last months of 1937, my mother says, were the darkest and saddest she had known. And her sadness coincided with a widespread anxiety that the Republicans were heading towards defeat.

3

Back in France, and settled in Toulon, Bernanos worked tirelessly on the final draft of *Les Grands Cimetières sous la lune*. Every day, the old, blue-eyed lion drove his motorbike to the Café de la Rade – not caring if the locals thought he was a drunk. There he finished his bleakest piece of writing.

Le Figaro newspaper published extracts of the book on April 16, 1938. By April 22, it was in the bookshops. The left-wing press commended him. The right-wing press either sulked or were downright hostile. In Madrid, the Spanish clergy demanded Bernanos' excommunication. His book, they said, had been inspired by none other than Satan. Simone Weil, a young philosophy teacher, wrote a letter of admiration to Bernanos that he kept in his wallet for the rest of his life.

Unable to chase the horrors of Spain from his mind, Bernanos decided it was time to up sticks again, but this time he wanted to go as far from his native country as possible. France, he said, had betrayed itself and Europe was embracing Totalitarianism. Staying put was unthinkable.

He spent his last evening on French soil with his wife and the writer José Bergamín. Bernanos and his family left Marseille on July 20. After a brief stopover in Dakar in Senegal, they sailed to Brazil and then on to Paraguay.

After the gloomy winter of 1937, Montse had no alternative but to take some kind of interest in life again. She had thought so much about José that she came to the conclusion his dying had perhaps in some mysterious way been desired. It had been a proud goodbye to a world José no longer belonged to, a world he had furiously rejected for some time because he refused to become like it, to reconcile himself to it – unlike Montse, who took the rough with the smooth and adapted and was even happy to do so. José's death seemed less absurd to her in this light. It was still as unacceptable, as pointless, but it was less absurd.

My mother has forgotten 1938 and the years that followed. Now I can rely only on books for information.

She has forgotten the small events (small in terms of History, those that are lost for ever) and the major events too (those I can still research).

She has forgotten how bad news darkened the Spanish skies in 1938 and how the Republican army continued to lose more and more ground.

She has forgotten that in March of that year the Naftali Botwin Company, made up of Jewish volunteers from all countries, was almost entirely wiped out in Lérida. She has forgotten how the big city where she experienced the happiest summer of her life, and probably her only happy summer, fell apart, the glorious banners and red posters of its desolate streets, like the spirits of its inhabitants, reduced to tatters.

She has forgotten how the Munich Agreement was signed that year, and how Daladier was applauded for his role in it (Jean Cocteau shouted, "Long Live the Shameful Peace!" A desperate Bernanos declared, "A shameful peace is no peace at all. We're drowning in shame, covering ourselves with it. It is an irredeemable shame and we will carry responsibility for it for the rest of time").

She has forgotten how on April 30, the Prime Minister of Spain, Juan Negrín, set up a coalition government. Its aim was no longer to defeat General Franco, but rather to enter into negotiations with him. Franco, obviously, refused.

In August 1938, the war came dangerously close to Montse's village. This was the Republican Army's last stand. A battle to the death had begun between the two sides in the village.

In February 1939, El Peque, the local roadman who had promoted himself to the role of town crier or *pregonero*, announced Franco's victory to all. The bonfire of hatred was lit and it spiralled out of control.

Changes in fortune were brutal, reprisals appalling.

Juan was executed. Two of Diego's assistants (neither of them yet eighteen years old) were tortured and shot. Carmen, the town hall secretary, and Rosita had their knees slashed and were ordered to wash the church floor on all fours. The building had not been used for three years and people crowded round to watch them, laughing thickly, spitting and hurling abuse. Many had swapped sides the night before and they shouted, *Long live Franco! ¡Arriba Franco! Long live Spain, ¡Arriba España!*, their arms and hands outstretched in an open-palm salute.

Manuel was locked up without charge in the prison of R. with a bunch of Andalusian Anarchists. They taught him to sing prison songs with melodies intended to make the heart bleed.

Bendición and her husband hung up a sign in their café. It stated:

WE WON'T SELL OUR COUNTRY TO FOREIGNERS.

Diego managed to get away in time to join General Líster's 11th Division as he retreated with his men to the French border.

At her husband's urging, Montse fled the village before reprisals began.

My mother left on the morning of January 20, 1939, pushing her daughter Lunita in a pram, carrying a small black suitcase packed with two folded sheets and a few of her daughter's clothes.

A dozen women and children walked with her. They converged with the long stream of people fleeing Spain, escorted by the 11th Division of the Republican Army. This was coyly known as *la Retirada*. It was, in fact, an interminable procession, a miserable column of old people, young women and children. Behind them, as they went, they left broken luggage, mules collapsed on their sides like discarded, muddied rags, the debris of possessions that had been grabbed in haste, precious fragments of a former home which were abandoned when the very notion of a home had disappeared from everyone's minds, when all ideas had evaporated. My mother walked for weeks, from dawn till dusk, wearing the same dress, the same jacket, stiff with mud. She washed in streams and wiped herself clean with the grass growing at the side of ditches. She scavenged what she could along the way or ate the odd handful of rice given to her by the soldiers of the Líster Division. All she thought about was putting one foot in front of the other and looking after her daughter who was having to endure this ordeal.

She soon gave up on the cumbersome pram and tied a sheet round her shoulders as a baby-sling instead. It became a part of her and she forced herself to walk on, stronger and freer, with her daughter held tight against her.

She was hungry and cold. Her legs, all her body, ached from head to toe. She slept without sleeping, her senses alert, her jacket folded as a pillow. She slept on the ground, on stacked branches, in abandoned barns, in empty, freezing schools, with women and children packed together so tightly it was impossible to move an arm without knocking against someone. She slept wrapped in a brown blanket too thin to keep out the dampness of the ground (my mother: *You know the one, the brown blanket, I use it on the ironing board*), her child hugged to her chest, both of them bound to each other as one body, one soul. *I'm not sure I would have made it without Lunita.*

Despite her youth, Montse had never known such tiredness. Still she carried on, putting one foot in front of the other, day after day, *ONWARDS!* Her whole spirit was fixed on survival, throwing herself on the ground or into a ditch as soon as any Fascist aeroplanes appeared, face squashed in the dirt, her petrified child pressed into her chest, breathless from crying, her child to whom she whispered, *Don't cry, my darling, don't cry, my sweetness, don't cry.* Each time she emerged from sheltering in a ditch, she wondered whether she'd been right to inflict this apocalypse on her daughter.

But Montse was seventeen and she wanted to live. She walked for days and days, her baby strapped to her, towards the other side of the mountain, where she believed life would be better. She walked for days and days through rubble and bombed-out stretches of land, reaching the border at Perthus on February 8, 1939. She was held in the concentration camp of Argelès-sur-Mer in appalling conditions, and then directed to the internment camp of Mauzac, where she was reunited with my father, Diego.

After further to-ing and fro-ing, she ended up in a village in the Languedoc where she learned a new language (which she soon deformed and massacred) and new ways of living and behaving. Most of all, though, she learned not to cry.

She still lives in the village to this day.

On April 24, 1939, His Holiness, the newly elected Pope Pius XII, stated:

IT IS WITH IMMENSE JOY THAT WE TURN TO YOU, DEAR SONS OF MOST CATHOLIC SPAIN, TO EXPRESS OUR PERSONAL CONGRATULATIONS

FOR THE GIFT OF PEACE AND VICTORY, GOD'S REWARD FOR YOUR HEROIC FAITH AND CHARITY.

February 8, 2011. My mother sits in the big green armchair next to the window overlooking the school playground. She is exhausted from telling me the story of her glorious summer. Her pride at describing it has drained her.

My mother has managed to preserve her most beautiful memories, still as raw as wounds. The rest, her other memories (with a few exceptions such as my birth), have been rubbed out. The entire burden of remembering has been wiped away. Seventy years, as unending as a Languedoc winter, have now vanished, fallen into silence, for reasons I still find hard to grasp. Medical reasons probably, or perhaps (and this theory of mine is more troubling) because these last seventy years have counted for nothing.

Only the summer of 1936 survives, a summer when life and love swept Montse away, a summer when she felt she was properly living for the first time, in harmony with the world, a summer of "total youth", as Pasolini might have put it. She lived, no doubt, in the shadow of that summer for the rest of her life. A summer, I presume, she embellished retroactively, rewriting the legend of it, the better to combat her regrets, unless it was to please me – as I have now safeguarded that remarkable season within these pages. For that is the purpose of books, too.

My mother's summer of glory, and Bernanos' year of sorrow, which remained fixed in his memory, a knife so deep it kept his eyes open: two episodes of the same past, two stories, two visions, which have haunted my days and my nights for months, slowly saturating them.

My mother stares out of the window, her one remaining pleasure. The playground empties of children.

It's very quiet now.

She turns to me.

Why don't you pour us an anisette, ma chérie? It would cheer us both up, give our morale a little boost. Is it le or la morale?

It's le moral.

A small glass of anisette is always a wise precaution, my Lidia. You've got to be prepared for anything in this day and age.

Glossary

Action Française: a far-right French political movement founded in 1899.

Anarchists: before the Spanish Civil War (1936–39), the Anarchist movement played an influential role in Spain, founding collectives and communes on agricultural land and introducing sweeping reforms in factories. From the summer of 1936 onwards, many villages lived as free, self-sufficient communes, stripped of all centralised control, without the presence of a police force or a judicial system.

Bernanos, Georges (1888–1948): Catholic and monarchist French writer. His book, *Les Grands Cimetières sous la lune*, documented Nationalist atrocities during the Spanish Civil War, particularly on the island of Majorca. (See author's preface.)

Carlists: proponents of *Carlismo*, an ancient, royalist and conservative political movement. The Carlists were supporters of Franco during the Spanish Civil War.

C.N.T. (*Confederación Nacional del Trabajo*): the National Confederation of Labour. Closely affiliated to the F.A.I. (see below).

Drumont, Edouard Adolphe (1844–1917): far-right, xenophobic French writer and journalist.

Durruti Column: the largest Anarchist military unit to fight Franco and the Nationalist forces. It was led by the Anarchist and syndicalist José Buenaventura Durruti Dumange (1896–1936).

F.A.I. (*Federación Anarquista Ibérica*): the Iberian Anarchist Federation.

Falange: a right-wing and traditionalist political movement founded in 1933. It gradually embraced Fascism and was later renamed *Falange Española Tradicionalista*. It became the official political party during Franco's dictatorship.

Franco, Francisco (General Francisco Franco Bahamonde, 1892–1975): leader of the Nationalists. On July 17, 1936, the Spanish garrisons in Morocco and the Canary Islands rose up against the democratically elected government of the Second Republic. General Franco became leader of the Nationalist insurgents and was given the name of *El Caudillo* ("The Leader") by his supporters. Franco believed resistance to his insurgency would evaporate within days, but Spain erupted into conflict. His followers became known as Francoists. Authoritarianism, nationalism and Catholicism were strong features of Francoism.

Hechos de Mayo: the violent events of early May 1937, especially in Catalonia, which pitted various left-wing factions against one another (chiefly Anarchists against Communists) in a battle to influence and control the revolutionary movement.

P.C.E. (*Partido Comunista de España*): the Spanish Communist Party. It supported the Republican forces.

P.O.U.M. (*Partido Obrero de Unificación Marxista*): the Workers' Party of Marxist Unification, founded in 1935 and opposed to Soviet-style Communism. George Orwell fought in its ranks during the Civil War.

P.S.O.E. (*Partido Socialista Obrero Español*): the Spanish Socialist Workers' Party.

Republicans: the forces of the Second Spanish Republic (1931–1939) were defeated by Franco's Nationalists, and the Republican government went into exile. The Republicans were generally supported by workers, trade unionists and small farmers, while large landowners, monarchists, the Roman Catholic Church and the army tended to back the Nationalists and Franco.

LYDIE SALVAYRE grew up near Toulouse after her exiled Republican parents fled Franco's regime. As a child she spoke Spanish, only learning French when she started school. She studied medicine and specialised as a psychiatrist in Marseille, before beginning to write at the end of the 1970s. Her novel *La Compagnie des spectres* won the Prix Novembre in 1997 and was named Book of the Year by Lire. *Pas Pleurer* (translated here as *Cry, Mother Spain*) won the Prix Goncourt in 2014.

BEN FACCINI is a writer and translator, born in England but brought up in France and Italy. He is the author of several books, notably *The Water-Breather* and *The Incomplete Husband*. In 2014, he was a contributing translator of *Outsiders*, a collection of short stories by Italian authors.